PAUL WRIGHT

HOW THE OTHER HALF DiES

A Summer Bailey Murder Mystery

For my wonderful children, Issy, Elliot, Anna and Katie-mae.
Proof that the seemingly impossible is achievable.

A wise man should have money in his head, but not in his heart.

JONATHAN SWIFT

Chapter 1

After

I stirred, listening. A moment's silence and then a wave slapped against the hull, making me jump and bringing me back to my surroundings. The last twenty hours filtered back in. How long had I slept? An hour? Amazing that I had managed to fall asleep at all.

As I opened one eye, I heard banging on the door. I rolled over and reached for the light above my head, feeling around for a switch. It was a hotel-style lamp with two switches beneath it, one to turn on the small lamp and the other to light up the room. I pressed both, squinting against sudden brightness. The cabin was suddenly revealed, the opulence of the yacht still surprising me.

I threw back the duvet and got out of bed, just as the knocking started again more insistently. I turned the lock and opened the door. Alice stood there. I reached up to hug her and she pulled me in close. We stood like that for several moments, holding one another. She laid her head on my shoulder, her long dark hair reaching down my back.

'I should have stayed with you last night, not left you on your own. Come and sit down,' I said, gesturing towards the small two-seater sofa by one of the portholes. Alice pulled me towards the bed, though, and sat me down on the edge, draping the duvet around our backs.

I looked at her eyes, devoid of makeup. Had I ever seen Alice without makeup before? Even back in college, when everyone was hard-up, dressed in hand-me-downs or cheap outfits bought at the market, Alice had been the elegant one. We never saw her looking anything less than spectacular. She always had amazingly manicured fingernails in the days before nails needed their own store. But now her eyes were puffy from tears, surrounded by dark shadows from lack of sleep. She looked quite broken – but then she would.

'I've been up all night.' She was trembling even though the air was warm.

'You should have stayed with me,' I repeated.

'I needed to be alone, to think, to try and get my head around this. I just needed a bit of space.'

'You're shivering. Look, let's get under the covers and see if you can't sleep here. We can talk in the morning.' I turned but Alice stopped me, gripping my arm, her eyes suddenly calm.

'What happened yesterday, it's all wrong.'

'I know it is,' I started to say, but Alice squeezed my arm harder.

'No, it really makes no sense. There's no way Jason killed himself. He loved me, he loved life too much. I need you to believe that. I need you to prove that.'

Chapter 2

Before

The doorman slid his scanner over the door-entry system, pushed open the door and stepped back to let us in. 'Mr Hanson will be here shortly, but he asked that you make yourself at home. Feel free to freshen up and help yourself to anything in the fridge. The coffee machine is set and ready to go,' he said as we moved past him, dragging our cases behind us.

Jason stepped in first and dropped the cases next to an elaborate, gold-plated tree-shaped coat stand. This wasn't his first visit. Alice and I followed him in, both stunned by the apartment.

In terms of size, the word 'apartment' didn't nearly describe the place. This was Monte Carlo, one of the most expensive areas of real estate in the world, and this apartment was enormous. The room we were in was the size of a tennis court. I was more used to eking out an existence in a small flat in West London, tripping over bits of furniture, with my bed pushed up against a wall to give me some floor space.

In the corner, a high-end Sonos speaker was quietly playing some easy-listening crooner. Alice looked at me and grinned, barely able to conceal her excitement. She mouthed, 'OMG.'

Jason pushed a button next to the coat stand and the shutters that had been protecting the apartment from the Mediterranean midday sun slid back silently, filling the room with brilliant sunlight.

Alice and I stood rooted to the spot, taking it in. Jason had told us that Mike's wife, Beth, had chosen every piece of furniture herself, all selected from Harrods during endless weeks, a shopping orgy. Looking around, I felt like I was in Aladdin's cave. Everything glittered. The sofa had an elegantly carved frame with an engraved motif at its centre of incredible workmanship; the frame was decorated in gold leaf and the piece was finished with sparkling gold cushions. To one side stood an oriental-style chest of drawers decorated with gold-lacquered cranes. I walked around the room, looking at each piece as if I were viewing a National Trust property.

The marble floor reflected a rectangular dining table that you would expect to have found in the Palace of Versailles. Jason saw me running my hand along the edge of it. 'That came from the Opera collection. It's a masterpiece, a reproduction that probably took longer to craft than the original. It's inspired by the fourteenth-century Florentine style. It would set you back the same as your apartment cost twenty years ago. This is how the other half live – for six months of the year, anyway.'

'Isn't this place incredible?' Alice cooed.

I smiled and nodded but kept quiet. It really wasn't to my taste at all. Money can buy you many things, but not great taste; for me, this place was the epitome of kitsch. Its garishness jarred and I found the overuse of gold leaf vulgar. They might live here for six months of the year, but it felt like a showroom rather than a home.

Hanging on the wall was a photograph of a group of men in cricket whites. They were posing in two rows, the front row sitting and the back row standing. In the centre, completely out of place in a pair of Bermuda shorts, sat a middle-aged man.

Jason joined me as I studied the picture. 'That's Mike in the centre, with the English cricket team. His greatest passion in life is cricket and he's very proud of his relationship with the English team. He knows all of the players personally and spends months every year, following them on their winter tour. We might be joining them for a few weeks of the journey, but Mike will spend the next few months following them around the Caribbean with his family and some friends. One long cricketing-holiday jamboree.'

As Jason wandered off, I looked more closely at the photo. I recognised a few of the faces from TV and the press. I wished I'd known about this passion of Mike's before we arrived. I could've read up on cricket so I wouldn't sound completely stupid in front of our hosts.

'There are a couple of bathrooms down here,' Jason called, 'if you want to freshen up before Mike arrives.'

'Gold-plated fittings, I assume,' I joked as I grabbed my case and headed for possibly the most luxurious shower of my life.

Chapter 3

After

I studied Alice's face, looking for signs that she didn't mean what she was saying, but her expression told me she believed it. For a moment I considered how to respond, how to be gentle with her without giving credence to this crazy, middle-of-the-night idea.

Jason had seemed worried; what with the scuba-diving, his accident and everything else he had going on, he obviously wasn't himself. If, in that moment, everything had seemed hopeless, then maybe…

'Summer, I know my husband,' Alice pleaded. 'Yes, he had problems this week, but nothing he couldn't have sorted out and got through. He was murdered by somebody on this yacht. Someone on here had reason enough to kill him. I need you to find out who it was before we get to Antigua because the police there won't want to get involved. They'll write it off as suicide.'

'I'm not the police,' I protested. 'I can't go around questioning people, I'm a guest here – and a guest of a guest, at that. I wouldn't know where to start.'

'Yes, but your programme – you're kind of a detective, aren't

6

you? You investigate stories, you dig into people's lives, get them to talk, get them to reveal secrets.'

When she said it like that, it did sound like I was some sort of detective – but that was really pushing the definition of detective. I presented a mildly popular TV show that had 'investigates' in the title. I made it look like it was me investigating everything, but the truth was that I had several researchers who did much of the work. They found the story, the characters. Maybe that was too modest, but I was no Miss Marple.

'You know I'm always here supporting you, Alice, and I'm someone you can talk to, but I can't help you with this. I'm not equipped to help. Jason's death will be looked into, it has to be. But what you're asking is something different.'

Alice got out of bed and crossed to a table. She popped the cap off a fresh bottle of water and poured herself a glass. 'We're in international waters on our way to Antigua, on a foreign boat with an English victim,' she said. 'Who do you think has the jurisdiction? Who will want to take this seriously? When Tom was killed in Gaza, you fought to get him justice. You were tenacious and battled for years. You know more about investigations involving foreigners abroad than almost anyone.'

Tom had been a BBC cameraman working on a story about education in Gaza when he was shot dead. We'd been married just five months when he travelled there as part of a team of four to document life in the refugee camps. On his final day, they'd been filming children throwing stones at the Israeli security forces after school finished, something that happened every day: school finished and the kids went out to throw stones before heading home for dinner.

Tom and the team were filming, wearing their standard

bulletproof 'PRESS' jackets and their blue helmets. It was just a normal day in Gaza... Suddenly a shot rang out. Tom was hit in the neck, between his helmet and the collar of his jacket. It was a single bullet that changed everything. They fought to save his life, there in the dust of Gaza, but it was hopeless. The bullet couldn't have hit anywhere worse.

I received condolences from the Israeli government and promises of an investigation, but it was all a whitewash. As the months went by, it became clear there would be no outside investigation. The Israeli army were satisfied that the shot had been fired in self-defence; the soldier who shot Tom said they were shot at first. Under attack by a mob that included terrorists, they had retaliated. His unit backed him up.

The aftermath dragged on for years. I wrote and met with the British government, imploring them to intervene and demand a full investigation, but it was clear they would only put limited pressure on an ally.

My involvement took me far out of my comfort zone. When Tom went to Gaza, I'd been freelancing for a magazine, writing fluffy pieces on business, dumbed-down articles so I didn't scare away readers who were more interested in gossip and fashion. One of Tom's colleagues, a producer called Terry who helped me tirelessly in my fight for justice, read one of my old articles and suggested I interview government representatives about the case on camera. He was making a documentary about Tom's death and thought the widow as an interviewer would be powerful stuff.

Naturally I was reluctant to begin with; I was a print journalist, happy to hide behind my keyboard. Stepping in front of the camera was a terrifying idea, but Terry assured me that I could do it. He told me to interview the minister just as

I interviewed businessmen when I was working.

The interview was awful. The junior Foreign Office minister was slippery and evasive and always had a seemingly perfect prepared excuse. He was called Hugo, and it was obvious that his public-school debating-society time hadn't been wasted. He was a natural politician, expert in saying nothing for long periods.

The interview was never used in the documentary but my frustration and anger at how Hugo got the better of me riled me. Terry was impressed with my style and how I'd handled the minister and asked me if I would do a piece on the plight of children living long term in bed-and-breakfast accommodation. The direction of my life changed at that moment in ways I had never expected.

'You're an outsider here, Summer, and you won't be seen as a threat. They'll talk to you. All you have to do is identify a suspect and the police can take care of the rest.'

Chapter 4

Before

With the midday sun streaming through the windows, I stood and looked down at the panoramic view of Monte Carlo. The Place du Casino was perfectly framed by the crystal waters of the Mediterranean behind it. Outside the casino, the area was bustling with tourists, cameras in hand, taking selfies with the Ferraris and Lamborghinis that had been parked in front of the casino to attract attention. All would-be Facebook posts for later, 'look at me with my other car'.

Behind me, the apartment door opened and a man entered. I knew this must be Mike, but he was not what I expected. Probably late fifties, slightly portly, wearing a T-shirt one size too large. Receding hair and salt-and-pepper stubble that had not been shaved for a couple of days. He looked like any other bloke his age and showed few signs of the wealth I knew he had. Only when you looked at his very worn casual clothing could you spot that it had come from a high-end boutique rather than a high-street store.

He saw me and smiled. 'Well, you must be Alice's friend – Sarah, is it? I'm Mike,' he beamed, his voice carrying his Black

Country origins.

'Summer,' I said as I put out my hand to shake his. I expected a bone-crushing experience but was surprised by the gentleness of his grip. 'It's good to meet you, Mike. I just want to say thank you so much for allowing me to join you on this trip.'

'Summer? What a gorgeous name. Well it's lovely to have you with us. Not a problem at all.'

Jason came in looking relaxed in a light-coloured, short-sleeved shirt and pale linen trousers. He gave a beaming smile. Jason was a couple of years older than me but could pass for twenty-five; his good looks and easy charm made quite a package.

'Mike, great to see you. You're looking well.' Jason and Mike didn't shake hands but grabbed each other and hugged.

'Good to see you guys, especially you, Alice, looking stunning as ever.' Mike kissed Alice lightly on each cheek. 'I'm so pleased you could make this trip. It should be a fantastic few weeks, a proper get away from it all.'

'It's incredible to be here, Mike,' Alice gushed. 'Your home is amazing. Beth has done a fantastic job finding such exquisite furniture. She must have a real eye for interior design.'

'She definitely knows what she wants. She loves to shop and, with years of practice, she's got it down to a fine art.' Mike headed towards the kitchen. Moments later he returned carrying the biggest bottle of Champagne I'd ever seen. 'It's after midday and you all must be parched. A drink to celebrate, and then I'm going to take you for a drive around Monte Carlo, if that's alright. It's no Birmingham, but it's home now for half the year. Have you ever driven the F1 circuit, Summer?'

As Mike poured pink champagne into my glass, the bubbles spilled over the lip of the glass and down my hand. 'No, I've not been to Monaco before, so I'd love to see some of the city before we leave,' I said, clearing the bubbles with a clumsy slurp.

'Fantastic. You're in for a treat. This might be a town full of billionaire tax exiles, but it still retains that Riviera charm. But first a toast, to us and our very good fortune.'

Chapter 5

After

I knew that sleep wouldn't return for me, so I left Alice sleeping soundly and headed out of the cabin. I followed the narrow corridor towards the stern. At the end of it, I passed the cabin where Jason and Alice had been staying. The door was open and the bed ruffled from her restless night.

Climbing a few steps, I went into the open, spacious TV room with its glass sliding doors that led onto the rear deck. I stepped out. Under the sunshade were a dozen canvas seats arranged around a central table. I sat on one and looked back to where it had happened, where Jason had taken his life – or so we all assumed.

At the back of the yacht stood a flagpole, the French flag fluttering gently in the gentle morning breeze. The sun had not yet risen; sitting there in the muted light, I looked at the pole and wondered what Jason had been thinking at that moment.

We'd been sailing around the clock, using the south-easterly wind to make up time on this doomed trip. Yasmin had been the one to find him after spotting the rope tied to the flagpole. She saw a shape in the water, bouncing along as the yacht cut through the Atlantic, travelling at a fair speed with the early morning wind. After helping the crew drop the sails to slow us down, she was able to pull the rope in.

Jason was being dragged behind the boat. The rope, a noose around his neck, was attached to the flagpole. He must have been in the water some time. I didn't see the body when it was first brought aboard, but later I saw the damage inflicted on his neck. It was substantial; it was amazing that the rope had not decapitated him.

He must have tied it around his neck and then climbed onto the chrome railing, the flag fluttering above him. How long did he sit there before throwing himself in? Did he ponder for ages, or throw himself straight off? He'd left no note; there were so many questions that might never be answered. I guessed it was possible that he'd fallen, slipped after changing his mind and tried to get back in. Or could Alice be right? Could he have actually been killed?

I walked to the flagpole and looked down. Directly below me was a jet ski, attached like a bike to a rack on a car. It would have been easy to jump clear of the jet ski but, if it were murder, how would they have attached a rope? How would they have made Jason sit on the rail and then forced him to jump clear? Or would the momentum of the boat have been enough to throw him clear? So many questions – but was I capable of answering them?

A sound behind me and I turned around to see Mike's daughter, Daisy, sliding open the glass door and stepping out. She was wearing a pink, fluffy dressing gown wrapped tightly against the morning chill. 'Can I join you?' she asked as she sat on one of the benches at the side of the boat. She pulled up her knees and hugged herself. 'We're not moving, are we?'

'No. I don't think anyone was up to sailing last night. Your dad said we need a break, the crew as well as us, so we heaved to and dropped anchor.' I took one of the chairs around the table and put my feet onto the chair next to me, letting my head slump back. We sat there for a few moments without speaking.

'Did you know Jason would kill himself?' asked Daisy in that matter-of-fact way the young do. Daisy was seventeen but could still be taken for a couple of years younger. Although she was developing the body of a woman, in the short time I'd known her on this trip she'd seemed childlike, living up to her position as the baby of the family. She was not allowed to grow up, and not pushing for it herself like most teenagers did.

'Of course not. Nobody could have, even those closest to him,' I said.

'I would have stopped him if I'd known. I'd have dragged him back into the boat myself.'

'You're a good person, Daisy. I'm sure you would have done everything you could to help. But he was obviously determined, waiting until the middle of the night like he did.' I stood up and moved towards her, then perched awkwardly on the edge of the bench and wrapped my arms around her. I felt something release in her, some pent-up emotion just waiting for a trigger to be released. She trembled and gave a little sob. I rocked her, as the ocean gently rocked us both.

'Jason was always funny with me. Not weird, but always making me laugh. I would have liked him to be my older brother.'

'He seemed very fond of you. Had you seen much of him before this trip?'

'When I was home from school, he sometimes came to Monaco to see Daddy about work and spent the night. I'm away at school for so much of the time, but I loved it when I got home and found him there. If he wasn't stuck with Daddy, he'd come and find me and talk. He used to ask me about school, how it was going, you know, like he was really interested.'

I shifted to make myself more comfortable and moved my back against the canvas sheeting that acted as a guard rail around this part of the yacht. 'I'm sure he loved talking to you, Daisy.'

She seemed genuinely upset about Jason, which was natural, but maybe more than she might have been about someone else. On this trip I'd got the feeling that Daisy wasn't very close to her parents. Mike seemed to love having his little girl around and gave her everything except the one thing she craved – his time. Beth was similar in many ways; to the outside world she was a mother who had seemingly dedicated her life to her two children, but Daisy seemed distant from her as well. I knew that sending children to boarding school was normal for the rich, but to me it seemed a cold way to treat children, even if they were sent to some incredible Swiss finishing school.

'Daddy will be upset, too, even though they'd been arguing.'

I sat still, my arms still wrapped around Daisy, then tried to ask casually, 'Your father and Jason had been arguing? What about?'

'I'm not sure. Money, I think. I heard Daddy shout "a lot of damn money" at him.'

'When was this, Daisy?'

'I don't know – maybe the night before the dive.'

Chapter 6

Before

Mike grabbed the bottle and gestured to us all to head out. 'Don't worry about your cases, they'll be sent down to the yacht. First, Monte Carlo!'

We went down to the garage under the apartment block. The ceiling was so low that Alice had to stoop to avoid the lights. Like the apartment, the garage oozed money. Cars were either red and sporty, or black with four fat wheels. There were a few vintage models thrown in, but generally it felt like walking through a sports-car dealership. Someone had parked a BMW i8 and probably felt ashamed every time they stepped out of their car.

We came to a Bentley that stood out because of its old-world elegance and styling. This was a car for royalty, not a flashy, brash plaything for the young or newly rich. It had a quiet sophistication. As we paused to admire it, even I felt a tingle of excitement; I'd never been in anything better than a stretch limo on a hen night.

'I've always driven a Bentley,' Mike told us. 'Nothing compares to them. And after the year I just had, I treated myself to this new beauty, the Bentley Bentaya. It's my one real indulgence in life, and this one is all thanks to Jason.'

'Pleased I could help, and you found somewhere worthwhile to put that cash, Mike.' Jason opened the rear-seat door to allow Alice to get in ahead of him. I entered through the opposite door and sank back into the soft tan-leather seat.

'You guys all good in the back?' Mike asked. 'I'll chauffeur. Glasses are in the back. Pour me one.'

I looked for a seatbelt, but Mike turned and said, 'You won't be needing one. These are safer than a tank. Just sit back and enjoy the ride.'

The car's engine was almost silent as he started it and pulled out of the garage into the brilliance of the Monte Carlo afternoon sun. I felt like a celebrity as I slipped my sunglasses back on and looked out upon the endless tourists milling about the city.

I glanced across at Jason and Alice, the perfect couple. Alice was striking; she looked like the proverbial sweet-faced girl next door, but her appearance hid a determined woman who got what she wanted. Jason was what she wanted; not only was he blessed with boyish good looks but he had charm and charisma and, best of all, he adored her. Every chance he got, he checked with Alice that she was okay and if he could do something for her.

Jason opened another bottle of champagne with the customary explosion of bubbles. He poured a glass for Alice first, one for me and then passed one up to Mike at the front.

'Is he alright with another? He's driving,' I whispered.

'Oh yeah, he's okay here.' Jason smiled. 'Monaco residents get special privileges. As long as he doesn't run over and kill another resident, the police won't give him a second look. It really is a different world here – that's why the rich and famous love it.'

As Mike and Jason talked football and the chances of Birmingham City ever reaching the big time again, Alice and I admired the beauty around us. We'd both come from a similar background – comprehensive school and bland housing estates, where ambition was in short supply and the locals' aspiration was to drive a decent car and buy a nice semi-detached in a cul-de-sac. We'd both had to battle our way out of the mire, never accepting a mediocre life for ourselves.

Alice had found her escape through acting and won a place on a drama course in spite of her family scoffing. I had discovered a love of writing and an interest in the financial pages of the newspaper from my dad when he worked for an insurance company. We'd both ended up going on to university, even though my careers' teacher had never mentioned it as an option. University wasn't meant for kids from my school, however bright they were. Against the odds, we'd both escaped to university: business studies and journalism for me, drama for Alice at the Bristol Old Vic.

Our lives now were far beyond what had been expected of us. No one in my class would have dreamt that I would ever be driven around Monte Carlo in a Bentley by a millionaire, even if it wasn't my own and it was just for a holiday.

We passed the principality's train station where we'd arrived just a few hours earlier. Because of Monaco's hilly location, the station has been built into the hillside, and rock and concrete combined in the very way that the principality did itself: old with new. Old and new were not always the best bedfellows, but Monaco managed to blend them beautifully.

'Do you watch the racing here, ladies?' Mike asked. 'We're now on what is the greatest street-racing circuit in the world.

It's hard to describe how this city is transformed on race day.'

As we passed elegant apartment buildings and drove down into Casino Park, we passed strikingly modern domes that rose up from the earth. Surprisingly, they housed a shopping centre rather than the modern art gallery that you might have expected. The narrowness of the roads struck me; I was in awe of the skill it would take to drive these streets at such high speed.

We moved down to a hairpin bend, passing another hotel that seemed to only serve those who drove supercars, and followed the road down towards the sea. Mike accelerated as the traffic cleared, pushing us gently back in our seats. Without that feeling of acceleration, I wouldn't have known that we were moving any faster because the car seemed to glide silently. There was no sound of air rushing past or tyres on the road. As we swept into the road tunnel, we seemed to levitate above the road in soundproof elegance.

I turned to Alice and mouthed, 'OMG.' Having never been too interested in cars other than in them getting me from A to B, I suddenly understood why somebody might spend a small fortune on one like this.

The harbour appeared as we emerged from the tunnel. The sun was blinding as it reflected off hundreds of impossibly white-and-chrome yachts moored in the vast harbour. Some of them were staggeringly large, of a size more suited to passenger ferries, their vast dimensions way beyond the needs of any man – and I was sure only a man would want one. They were designed and built only to portray the wealth and power of their owners. Their crews were in military-style white suits, engaged in an endless round of cleaning and polishing, always ready for the whim of the owner to call them into service.

The smaller boats and yachts looked cute next to their flashier neighbours. These were status symbols for hedge-fund managers and bankers. Nothing said you'd made it like a powerboat at Monte Carlo. The mooring fees alone would keep out all but the wealthiest boat owner.

'So, Mike, which one of these is yours?' asked Alice, leaning forward in her seat.

'The *Althea* is moored just along the next stretch. You won't be able to see her from the road, but if you knew where to look you might just see the tips of her masts. Have either of you sailed before?'

Alice and I looked at one another and smiled.

'If you count sailing in dinghies on Lake Windermere, then we have,' Alice said. 'We spent a wet, blustery weekend of adventure in the Lake District when we were seventeen, with two guys who thought they could impress us with their "boat". A disastrous weekend, wasn't it, Summer?'

I grinned at her as I recalled the awfulness of that May weekend spent in mist and drizzle with two guys who were as wet as the weather. 'No one drowned, but throwing myself overboard would have been tempting had Alice not been there.'

'I knew then I wasn't cut out for a life of hostel holidays with cheap gin and tonics,' Alice laughed. 'After that weekend, we got summer jobs and saved until we could afford a fortnight in Corfu. Our first time abroad, and a slice of a life that was far more to our taste. It was a package holiday, and we were surrounded by families, but at seventeen we felt like we were jetsetters, drinking cocktails at beachside bars.'

Alice continued with tales of our previous holiday; it seemed a lifetime ago but, in hindsight, it was tremendously important to us both. It was a turning point when we realised that life had more to offer than suburban living and the repetition of work, home and one holiday a year. We met guys that week who lived that mediocre life, for whom this one fortnight was the highlight of the year. They were in a desperate rush to sleep with as many girls, drink as many beers and get as brown as was humanly possible before returning to the factory or building site where they slogged away for another year and counted down the weeks until they could repeat it all again. That week, we knew we wanted more, Alice especially.

I had admired Alice for her ambition and was envious that she had a goal that still eluded me. While I knew I desired a better life, the path was not clear to me at that point. As we sat on the beach, sipping two-for-one margaritas, she sneered at the other girls and pitied their small lives and lack of ambition. She was going to be somebody, to drink cocktails not with the tattooed masses that surrounded us but with the beautiful people, the wealthy and educated who would appreciate her beauty and elegance and hang on her every word. Acting was to be her escape from herself into a character that she would create to fit the life she craved.

We continued driving away from the marina, sliding around the corners and hairpin bends as we climbed the hillside that gave us ever-greater views of Monte Carlo below. I looked at Alice as she watched Jason. We'd hardly seen each other in the years since college but, here and now, it looked as though all of those dreams from Corfu had come together for her.

Chapter 7

After

Mike and Jason had argued about money, possibly the night before the scuba dive. After Daisy dropped that little nugget, she left in search of warmth. Alone again, I found that I was staring vacantly at the flag that now lay limply, the slight breeze having fallen away completely.

Alice's wild ideas about Jason looked just a little less fantastic after hearing that Jason and Mike had argued. I needed coffee, a shower and then a talk with Alice.

She was still in my bed, her back turned from me as I crept in. I couldn't see if she was sleeping or not, so I set her coffee down on the table next to my own and went into the bathroom. Small and a little cramped, it was still the height of luxury with an impressive power shower that would help to clear my head.

I was standing under the shower, letting the jets pound my skull and thinking back over my conversation with Daisy, when the bathroom door opened and Alice stepped in. Through the frosted glass, she looked much brighter than earlier and she directed a half smile at me. Pulling up her dressing gown and sweeping it around behind her, she sat on the toilet to pee with no hint of embarrassment about her nakedness or mine.

'Sorry about last night. I just had to say it, to know that you knew, in case something happened to me as well.'

I cut my shower short. Wrapping a towel around me, I stepped past her into the cabin. Talking through the door now, I said, 'Alice, you're being paranoid. Nothing is going to happen to you. I'm not sure anything *happened* to Jason, but I'm sure you're perfectly safe.'

She came out of the bathroom, crossed the room and hugged me. 'Jason didn't kill himself, which means somebody on this yacht did. Until you can find out who that was, I'm not going to feel safe. You can solve this – find out who killed Jason.'

I smiled and made vague promises to do all I could, even though I felt no confidence in my words. Alice sat at the small table next to the porthole and picked up her coffee as I started to dress.

'This can wait if you don't want to talk now, but what exactly did Jason do for Mike?' I asked. I hadn't pried before now, which seemed strange in hindsight. I had agreed to this trip with Alice, and I'd accepted that Jason worked for Mike in some financial capacity; I'd just assumed that free holidays on luxury yachts were thrown into the bargain.

'He worked on Mike's behalf, moving money around and investing and trading for him. He kept Beth and Mike very comfortable. Jason had a knack for it – he always had. If he'd had his own large sum of money to invest, we'd be the ones living in Monte Carlo. But money goes to money, and you need plenty to even get to the table. You don't get to play at this level without starting with a million. Thanks to the profits Jason was making, though, we were just getting to a position where he could invest for us. He was ready to place his first bets.'

I opened the wardrobe to select a dress to go over my bikini. I felt I should wear black, something dignified, but I'd only packed light and airy clothes. 'So how did Jason meet Mike?'

'Jason was working for an investment company. He was only a junior, but he had the rare talent of being both technically brilliant and a people person. Most technical analysts you meet are financial geeks – they can't read a spreadsheet and hold a conversation at the same time. Jason was always charming and confident with people, so he was often used to drum up business, find new clients. He was soon earning good money, getting share bonuses for every client he brought to the company. His skill of explaining the company's investment strategy in plain English meant he was more useful to the company travelling the world and winning new clients than he was in front of a computer screen. Mike was down in Antibes, at an investment conference not far from Monaco.'

'So Jason met Beth and Mike at an investment conference?'

'Really?' said Alice, with her 'you must be kidding face'. 'Beth would have been there for the Gucci handbags and chic jewellers, not some dull conference. The place stinks of money and Beth loves the smell. I don't know the details of how Jason and Beth met. You'll need to ask Beth.'

Alice was sneering about Beth and her love of money, but was she any different? She envied Beth this life, wanted it for herself. For Alice, this trip had been a test run to experience how the other half lived before she joined them.

This was the life she'd planned with Jason, and it had been cruelly ripped away from her. Without Jason, she could never reach these heights. She'd inherit from him, of course; there would be life insurance and the home in Kew Gardens could be paid off. Alice would still live a life most people could only dream about, but I could see that she wouldn't be content. She had been too close to all this.

'Jason bumped into them both again at the Geneva motor show. Mike was there for the launch of some new model of Bentley. They got talking football – Mike has a lifelong love of Birmingham City, and Jason could feign interest in anything if needs be. Mike had a corporate box at the ground and invited Jason to join him. Less than a year later, when the financial crisis hit, Jason's company got badly burned. Within a week of Lehman Brothers' collapse, it was liquidated. We lost almost everything overnight, not just Jason's job but all the shares Jason had built up in the company. We'd just moved into the house in Kew with an eye-watering mortgage, and suddenly we faced losing it all. I had to give up acting just as I was about to break through, and I was working in deli six days a week. Jason struggled for a while to find a way back in via his old contacts. Investment analysts weren't in high demand just then.

'Mike and Beth lost money in the collapse as well, but not too much. Mike is careful with his money, careful not to put all his eggs in one basket, and he needed someone he could trust. He stayed in touch with Jason and saved us just when things were looking most bleak because my salary wouldn't cover the mortgage, let alone the bills. We were drowning under the weight of a mortgage on a house worth less than we'd paid for it.

'Jason went down to Monaco, his one last throw of the dice. He maxed out our credit cards so he could head down to Monte Carlo to try and get his own business off the ground. He met with Mike and explained how he could use the financial crash to Mike's advantage. The US government was starting to print

26

money and that would hit the value of the dollar. Jason said he could take advantage of that for Mike with almost no risk because this was about investing in currencies, and currencies didn't go bust.'

I joined Alice at the table and sipped my now-cold coffee. 'So Mike just trusted Jason with his millions?'

'They were rich by our standards, but Mike wasn't super rich, and he was cautious because he'd already lost money in the crash. He offered Jason a few hundred thousand to invest for him, maybe half a million. It was a tiny amount really, but it was enough for Jason to work with. He was transformed after a year of stress. He worked all hours, often through the night because his investments were often based on currencies that were dealt during the night on the Asian markets. You'll understand it better than me. But the investments paid off, and in the first year Jason's commission was enough to get us back on our feet. As time went on, Mike increased his investments. The profits kept coming, Mike's wealth grew and we benefited as well.

'Mike helped Jason win some other customers, retired British tax exiles with their millions, successful in their businesses but clueless about investing. Jason reassured them, took their money and grew it. Last year was a good one. He made big profits for Mike, which is why we're here. It was supposed to be a luxury thank you.'

Chapter 8

Before

We arrived at the marina and went down walkways between gleaming yachts. Most of them were closed up but a few had small groups enjoying lunch. The smell of barbecued seafood and steaks mingled with the scent of a marina, that slightly stale ocean smell where the water sits just a little too long without moving.

As we cornered the walkway, we saw our yacht moored to one side, pointing outward, ready for departure. With two huge masts, *Althea* sat high in the water. Her royal-blue hull made her look majestic amid the ultra-modern speedboats, and her old-world beauty invoked images of a more stylish era, of movie stars and starlets oozing sophistication.

As we approached the gangway, we were met by a striking woman with wonderfully olive skin and long curled locks. 'Good to see you, Mike. Everything is ready, and nearly everyone has arrived. Charlie and Jane are onboard, and we are just waiting for Nicholas,' she said as she shook his hand, maintaining eye contact with him. As the handshake broke, she turned to smile at the three of us.

'Welcome aboard the *Althea*. She's maybe not the largest but she's certainly one of the most stunning yachts in the Med, although I am slightly biased.' I tried to place her accent: not native French. Judging by her complexion and hair, I guessed she came from a former French colony for she spoke English with a French accent, mixed with somewhere else – Morocco or Tunisia, maybe. She had the most brilliant green eyes, bright and soft all at the same time.

'Is this a schooner or a yacht?' asked Alice.

'Technically this is a schooner because the after mast is higher than the foremast, but nobody says schooner – it sounds too Aussie. Around here, it's just a yacht.'

'This is Yasmin, our captain,' Mike said. 'A most able seaman and, as you can see, knowledgeable on all things nautical. Yasmin, this is Jason, his wife, Alice, and her friend, Summer.' Yasmin moved along the line, shaking hands with each of us. 'Yasmin, maybe you could introduce the crew as well?' he added.

'Of course.' Yasmin turned to the three impeccably dressed crew standing awkwardly beside her on the deck, trying to look smart without standing to attention as if they were in the Navy. 'We have Louis, our chef for this voyage. It's his first time with us, but he's worked on some of the most luxurious yachts in the Med serving the finest French cuisine. Or a full English breakfast, if that's what you desire.' She smiled as she directed the comment at Mike.

'Then we have our crew, Lotte from The Netherlands, who speaks English better than I do, and Martina from Tuscany who will take every opportunity to practise her English on you. Lotte and Martina will assist you in any way possible. They will act as crew as well as waiting on you and keeping your home spotless for the next few weeks.'

I looked at the three of them, this international crew that was here to cook and clean for us while we … while we did what? I hadn't really thought about how I would spend my time for the next four weeks; I'd naively thought we would be helping out around the boat, assisting with the sailing, cooking a meal. Instead we would be waited on hand and foot and we wouldn't have to lift a finger. I had a sudden panic that I hadn't packed enough books for the trip.

The crew stood there in their starched white outfits, the women wearing shorts and white pumps while Louis wore long, rather baggy trousers. They were all older than I'd expected. I still assumed crewing a yacht was a gap-year job, but they were all a good ten years older than me, so I assumed they were career crew. Lotte, the Dutch women, had her blonde hair pulled back tightly, drawing her features tight. Martina was much darker and had her hair cut into a long bob that reached just above her shoulders.

'It's time we went aboard and met everyone else. They'll be wondering where we've got to.' Mike led the way and we followed him up the gangplank where we shook hands with the crew, leaving me strangely self-conscious.

We walked towards the bow and entered the boat via a large sliding door. The yacht was far more spacious than it appeared from outside. There was a small, raised gallery area with polished wooden flooring furnished with seats that looked out towards the front of the boat; protected from the elements, it was a perfect position to sit and enjoy the view. If we hit a storm, I would be there in the front-row seats to enjoy the show.

I had worried that Alice would have to duck down inside but even the gallery had a high ceiling. This upper area was framed by a glass banister, with a staircase going down into a wide room. There were crisp white sofas and a large table with a beautiful display of lilies at its centre. A large-screen TV dominated one wall; it looked slightly out of place and spoiled the stylish look of the room.

'Your cabins are down these stairs, through the back here. Your bags will be brought to your cabins for you. Let's find the others and I'll show you where you're staying.' Mike led us through the living area into a corridor that had several doors before coming to some stairs leading down to a lower level and another corridor. He pointed. 'This is the master cabin. There's more space than we need, but Beth loves the light in here. She often sits and paints by the window.'

I peeked through the open door into a beautifully furnished living room with two bedrooms leading off it. In one of them I saw an en-suite bathroom reflected in a mirror and a deep walk-in wardrobe filled with an expensive array of summer dresses. It was tasteful, nautical, with its navy blues and whites; there was none of the garish gold here. Over by a large window stood an easel and a blank canvas primed and ready, with a painter's stool next to it. It was strange to see two bedrooms leading off from the living area.

'This is all so incredible, Mike. Absolutely beautiful, all of it,' cooed Alice.

'Well, this is home on and off for the next three months, so we need a few creature comforts. I thought Beth would be in here though. Beth?' Mike called down the corridor.

A door opened and a woman stepped out, a glass of sparkling wine in her hand. 'We're all in here, Mike. We started the party without you!'

Mike approached her and they embraced. She kissed him

31

very tenderly on one cheek as she held him for a moment. She was a plain woman with a pale, lightly freckled complexion. She wore a pair of heavy pink glasses that clashed with her bright red hair. She was a similar age to Mike and had the same strong Black Country accent.

'Everyone, this is one of my oldest friends, Jane. And no, I don't mean oldest!' Mike winked.

Jane punched him on the arm in that friendly way that only close friends have. 'Thanks for that. I think it's obvious that I'm not the oldest anything.' She turned and led us into the cabin. It was similar to the other one though slightly smaller, decorated in the same nautical manner, with a painting of a beach scene with local fisherman pulling in a catch hanging over the bed.

Another woman was sitting by the window. She was attractive; her long chestnut-brown hair reflected the sunlight flowing through the window, and she was wearing a striking designer dress with a plunging neckline. She was younger than the man opposite her – she looked to be in her mid-forties thanks to her vibrant choice of hair colour, but she was probably closer to fifty. I thought she must be Mike's wife, Beth, and the man must be Jane's husband, Charlie. He had a kind, affable face, with a broad smile beneath his moustache.

They both stood, smiled and walked towards us. Mike did the round of introductions and we exchanged air kisses, handshakes and compliments.

Charlie seemed to radiate warmth as he greeted us. He had that distinguished look of a solicitor, someone who'd retired early from an office job. The skin on his hands was soft and delicate, starting to thin with age. Beth seemed genuinely thrilled to see us as she greeted Jason warmly with a long hug before hugging both Alice and me.

Alice seemed just a little stiff as Beth pulled her in, her smile a little forced. She had always had something of a problem with women she saw as more attractive than herself. When I'd first realised this at college I'd been hurt for a while, what with Alice being completely relaxed with me. We'd never discussed it, but I always knew when we met new people if she would warm to them or not. She loved to be the centre of attention and spurned those who could pull the spotlight from her.

'Lovely to see you again, Alice.' Beth smiled at her warmly. 'And I'm so pleased you could join us as well, Summer. I look forward to getting to know you.'

'Can you call Nicholas, please, Beth? I told him I wanted to make a sharpish getaway.' Beth pulled out a gold sparkly cased phone that matched perfectly with her glittery nail polish and started to dial while Mike turned to Jason. 'We have dinner booked and you're all in for a treat. Now, where's that bubbly?'

Chapter 9

After

The yacht had a data link via satellite, giving us access – albeit slow access – to the outside world. I had avoided it for most of our trip, using the isolation at sea as the perfect excuse to shut myself away from the world. The control room had a laptop that Yasmin used to stay up to date with the latest weather forecasts and assist with navigation. I had assumed professional captains still used charts and compasses to guide them, but it seemed that Yasmin was part of a new breed that relied on tech. Even though she kept a few old maps and charts in the control room for show, I had never seen her look at them; she always used her mobile device with its nautical satnav to guide us.

The screen was full of various weather maps and mapping tools, far more detailed than I was used to. The view was confusing, but we seemed to be sailing in settled conditions. There were no more terrifying storms on the horizon, at least in the immediate future.

I flicked around looking for a browser window, not wanting to shut any open windows. I opened a new tab and then closed it before opening an incognito window. It was still early so there was little chance of anyone walking in on me, but I didn't want to leave any history of what I was looking for – even if my search was innocent.

In the search bar I typed David Hanson Construction, the name of the company Mike had sold. After a brief pause, the screen filled with results. I scrolled down the list and read the snippets of information that the search engine had thrown up. Most of the posts were news pieces, charity events, business reviews, nothing of any interest.

I wanted the financial results, so I added the word 'purchase' to the search bar. A new page appeared with headlines that sounded more interesting: *Tyler Housing plc completes purchase of David Hanson construction.* I opened the article from the financial pages of the *Birmingham Post*; it had been written nearly ten years ago.

Tyler Housing plc yesterday completed its purchase of Birmingham-based construction firm David Hanson Construction for £67 million in cash and shares. David Hanson started the company bearing his name at the end of WWII, buying up bombed areas of Birmingham for next to nothing and building cheap housing for the large number of people made homeless during the war. The business grew quickly, becoming the number one housebuilder during the 1960s.

The company continued to enjoy success until the bitter recession in the 1980s forced it to sell off much of its business. The housing boom of the late 1980s saw a revival of its fortunes, although the company was much smaller than in its 1960s' heyday.

With his son Mike now involved, David stepped back. The business moved beyond housing construction and into office and retail construction, culminating in the building of Lockhart Tower, at the time the tallest building in the city. The timing was poor, however, and another recession in the early 1990s rendered the Lockhart Tower a white elephant. It sat empty for many years, draining the business of vital capital.

The near-collapse of the business led to David's return on a day-to-day basis. He steadied the ship before rebuilding the company again by buying up brownfield sites that were no longer required due to the industrial decline of the area.

By the time David retired again, this time for good in 2001, the company was back on its feet and building hundreds of houses a year across the Midlands. Mike Hanson continued running the business until his father died in 2006. Almost immediately afterwards, Mike hired Decca & Co as business advisors to find a buyer. This culminated in yesterday's sale of David Hanson Construction to Tyler Housing, ending almost sixty-five years of housebuilding by the Hanson family.

I closed the tab and checked the history to make sure I'd left no trace of what I was looking at. It wasn't that I felt I had done anything wrong, but I was uncomfortable about looking into my host. There was no trace of my search but, as I scrolled down through the history, a line caught my eye: *Death at sea and jurisdiction for investigations*. The article had been viewed five days earlier, four days before Jason's death.

Chapter 10

Before

U sing the motor, Yasmin eased us gingerly out of the harbour. The entrance to the marina was bustling, with boats coming and going through the narrow entrance. We were out on the deck watching our departure, sipping yet another glass of pink bubbly, when Daisy came out to join us. She looked very much a child at a grown-ups' party as she ran up to Jason and gave him a massive hug. She kissed Alice and then introduced herself to me by throwing her arms around me. The alcohol and sun had combined to leave me unsteady on my feet as she released me.

Daisy was a breath of fresh air. She was wearing a brilliant-pink bikini that showed off her young curves perfectly, especially as she carried a bit of teenage weight. Her blonde hair was sun streaked and her delightful round face full of smiles.

Although I was nearly ten years older than her, she seemed to gravitate towards me, maybe sensing that I would be some younger company. As we motored away from Monaco and headed along the coast towards France, she chatted away at me as if we'd known each other for years.

Barely drawing breath, she said, 'For my eighteenth, Mummy

said I could bring any singer I wanted to play at my party. Who would you have? Do you think Ed Sheeran would play? I saw him at Glastonbury last year. We had VIP passes, so I saw him from the side of the stage. He would be awesome, wouldn't he?

'No, it's an all-girls school in Geneva, set in the mountains, looking down over the water fountain – more *The Sound of Music* than Hogwarts, worse luck. But we still get up to stuff. You know, we have *real* nuns there. They don't know what we get up to sometimes –it's so funny.

'I'll probably go to university in England, or maybe America. Most of the girls are going to England, but Sunni – she's my best friend – she's off to Berkeley, which is in America somewhere, and I might go with her…'

I warmed to Daisy straight away. She was a sweet girl, but also immature. She was probably the mostly widely travelled teenager I'd ever met, but she lived in a bubble of privilege that kept her cocooned from the real world. She seemed to have no concept of money or how life was for most people. But, with all her parent's money, would she ever need to know these things? The chances were that she would move through life as she was doing now, seeing the world from the deck of a yacht or the back of a Bentley.

After a couple of hours of sailing, and in quieter waters, Yasmin and the crew lowered the sails and we started to slow before they dropped the anchor. Attached to the back of the yacht and hoisted out of the water was a jet ski, the only real rich playboys' toy that seemed to be allowed on this otherwise elegant yacht. Yasmin started to lower it while Mike announced we would be stopping for a few hours of playtime.

Daisy jumped up and grabbed Jason. 'Come on, Jason, us first. Who's driving?'

Jason grinned, as he lifted her in a fireman's hold and threw her over the side of the yacht. Alice and I looked over just as Daisy surfaced, laughing and wiping the water from her face. 'Okay – for that, I'll be driving first. You're probably drunk anyway!'

She set off to swim around to the jet ski and climb aboard. Jason dived in and swam after her, clambering on awkwardly behind her as she started up the engine. With a shower of water, Daisy roared off, leaving him to cling on, whooping and cheering as they bounced across the gentle waves.

Although we were all pretty tipsy, the cool water was too inviting after lying around on deck for hours. One by one we dived in and spent a glorious couple of hours swimming and taking it in turns on the jet ski.

Just as we all seemed to be winding down and were returning to the deck for fruit juices and shade, Mike appeared on deck with water skis. After attaching them to the jet ski, he took Daisy out for a spin. They raced around the yacht in circles, twisting and turning so she could jump the small waves made by the jet ski. She was amazingly graceful and completely confident on the water; obviously, her years of skiing on both snow and water were paying off.

After Daisy had finished her performance, Alice, Jason and I embarrassed ourselves in front of Mike and Daisy. Simply standing upright and moving in a straight line was tricky, and I found it exhausting constantly pulling myself back up out of the water every thirty seconds. Jason and Alice seemed to get the hang of it after a few minutes and soon looked confident.

A boat passed us carrying tourists along the coast and the passengers looked over at us on our yacht, water skiing or lounging around in the sun drinking cocktails. If I'd been passing by, I would have been so jealous of these rich young playthings living a life I could only dream about. Yet at this moment I was here, with Alice, experiencing the life that we had only dreamt of. Would I miss this when it was over, when I was back on the tourist boat looking on? Probably.

After we were exhausted with playing, we sailed on for several hours. The French coast was always in sight, the long esplanade of Nice beyond its airport jutting out into the sea. As we approached Antibes, the lights reflected on the calm waters as the sun began to set over the Mediterranean. Everyone slowly disappeared, leaving me alone to enjoy the tranquillity. I was still buzzing from the champagne and I smiled to myself as I watched France drift by.

When Alice and I had met nearly ten years earlier our families had given us few expectations about how life would unfold for us; yet, when I looked back, maybe we were destined to arrive here. My quiet ambition to carve out the life I wanted had been there from a very young age. Alice had never hidden her ambition; it was there for all to see. She always said that if you acted as if you were a success, people would believe you were and treat you as a winner.

I had found my niche through tragic circumstances but, in those moments when I dwelt on my life with Tom, I felt that something would have happened anyway. Alice had never expected my minor television success. The truth was that she loved having me around at college as her less successful sidekick, someone a little less than her – a little less attractive, less clever, less gregarious.

I'd been surprised when she'd invited me on this trip. It was last minute, so maybe she was casting around for someone to keep her company and I was free. Who else could drop everything for a month at short notice? My next project had been greenlit, but we weren't starting on it for another two months and I'd been thinking about getting away for a long-overdue holiday. Whatever the reason, I was thrilled by the invitation. Although I often investigated and interviewed the rich through my work, to hang out with them and see their life from the inside was a chance I couldn't resist.

Jason came on deck wearing stripy blue-and-white shorts with matching sliders, holding his phone and waving it around as he searched for a signal. He saw me and smiled as he came over. 'No signal here and we're only a few miles offshore. I'm not sure how I'll survive once we get to the ocean.' He slid the phone into his shorts' pocket, looking very much the college prep kid at sea. 'So, this is how the other half lives. You could get used to this, couldn't you?'

'It would certainly be good to have the choice – although I'm not sure I could get used to having quite so much wealth.'

'I know what you mean. Money is a double-edged sword sometimes. I went to a private school and most people were nice enough, but those who came from money were a breed apart from those of us on scholarships or whose parents had spent their last penny on school fees.'

'Was it worth it though, education-wise, I mean? I went to a comprehensive and never wanted to go private, but I was jealous of the better education that seemed to be available to those lucky few.'

'Private school taught me to speak well, to mix with privilege. It forced me to work harder than I might have done in a normal school, but it didn't leave me any smarter. Sometimes I'm jealous of Alice and her schooling. It toughens you up when you have to fight to be heard and to learn.'

41

'Our upbringing certainly wasn't easy. Alice always knew she wanted something. Thanks to you, she has. You seem very happy. I'm glad she found you.'

'That's a lovely thing to say, Summer. We're lucky to have found each other. Alice is a special woman, and I don't know what I'd do without her. The first time I saw her, I knew I'd found the one – waking up with her every day is a privilege that I am always thankful for. We make a team in life that I could only dream of before we met. She's supported me and pushed me to achieve so much more than I would have otherwise. If it weren't for Alice, we wouldn't be here today enjoying Mike and Beth's fantastic hospitality. *She* made this happen. It's all thanks to having Alice in my life.'

Jason's phone began to buzz in his pocket. He pulled it out and looked down, using one hand to reduce the glare. I watched him as he squinted, his forehead creasing as he read whatever was on the screen. His face became pained. He looked up at me. 'Sorry, I have to go deal with something, just boring work stuff. I'll see you later.' His attempt to sound upbeat didn't match the grave expression on his face.

As Jason departed, he passed Charlie and Jane who were coming up onto the deck. Jane was wearing a sparkling evening gown with a large bead necklace, and Charlie was dressed in a smart jacket with a starched white shirt. They offered greetings to Jason as he passed, but his head was down and it looked as though he hadn't heard them.

'Are you not getting changed, my dear? We'll be eating soon,' said Charlie.

My sun-soaked, glowing smile must have dropped as I suddenly felt very sober and very underdressed. While I'd been enjoying the French Riviera, the others had slipped away to change into chic evening wear. I was still in the simple white cotton dress that I'd been wearing over my bikini. A great first impression I was going to make.

Behind me I heard the rumble of a large outboard motor. A wooden motorboat was heading towards us. Delaying everyone while I got changed would make a bad impression, so I decided to go with it.

Jane said kindly, 'You're looking lovely, Summer, like a movie starlet straight out of Cannes. The advantage of being young is that you look fabulous wearing anything or nothing.'

'Jane!' Charlie admonished. 'Sorry, my wife gets a little frisky when she's had a few too many bubbles.'

The boat drew closer. There were lights from a small rocky island just behind it, while Cannes in the background illuminated the sky, creating a glow around the island. Other yachts and power boats were moored offshore, swaying in the moonlight.

Yasmin caught the rope and eased the boat alongside before lowering a ladder. I was the first to climb down, Charlie's warning to be careful ringing in my ears.

'Bonsoir, madame. Bienvenue à *La Gayleata*,' said the driver as he took my hand and helped me descend. I took a seat towards the back on a well-padded cushion and looked up, just as Alice and Jason came out. Jason grinned down at me and Alice gave me a wave, her eyes bright and full of excitement.

Chapter 11

After

Mike was standing at the bow of the yacht looking out to sea as I came up on deck. 'Summer, come see,' he called as he saw me approach. Below us, a small pod of dolphins was bow riding just below the surface of the water, twisting and turning as they rode the waves we'd created. As they powered through the water at a fair rate of knots, sometimes one would leap up and turn on its back before diving back under. I grabbed the mast pole and sat on the edge of the boat, mesmerised by their play as they crossed back and forth over one another, surfacing every minute or so for a second to catch a breath before dropping down again.

'They're like kids bodyboarding, playful and carefree,' Mike said. 'I could watch them for hours. Completely takes your mind off things.'

'I can imagine. This must be a really hard time for you. Losing Jason like that is horrible for all of us, but you were particularly close to him.'

'I was, yes. He was more than just a business acquaintance – I don't take all my business associates away with me. We were friends, even with everything that went on during this trip.'

Mike looked as though he was going to say something more but stopped himself.

I looked back at the dolphins and considered if I were in a position to ask questions. 'I don't want to pry,' I said slowly, 'but I would like to understand why Jason might have felt desperate enough to take his own life. Was he having a problem with the money he managed for you?' I was unsure if I had overstepped the mark and how Mike would react.

He let out a big sigh. 'Jason has done some great work for me. It seemed he always had the Midas touch. As I've said, he did well and made good returns – at least until this past week, when he lost it all, and more.'

'In just a week?'

'In just a day – an afternoon. It seems that getting it wrong coincided with a massive bet, one I knew nothing about. It was a bet that offered fantastic profits but equally fantastic losses. In just a few hours, his million-pound trade lost me millions.'

I watched Mike as he spoke, trying to gauge how bad this was for him. How many millions had he lost, and how did he feel about it? As I started to speak, two dolphins leapt together, crossing each other in the air before diving again. Mike grinned like a child, pleasure etched on his face. However bad things were, he hadn't lost his sense of wonder.

I pressed on. 'How could his bet have lost so much? Surely if you bet a million, you lose a million?' I'd found that playing dumb always seemed to be a good policy when you wanted to get people to open up.

Mike turned to look at me, assessing me, deciding how much to say. His shoulders sagged and he blew out some air. 'You seem to have hit on the problem. I don't really understand it myself, and I'm angry that I didn't take more interest in

45

what Jason was doing and what risks he was taking. He was betting on currencies, predicting whether or not the value of the currency would be higher or lower tomorrow, next week or in a month. Currencies are like shares. They go up and down in value based on a million things. Unlike a share in a company, though, currencies are linked to nations and therefore their value doesn't change enormously from one day to the next. The value changes over time, but day to day those changes are hardly noticeable. Not normally, anyway.

'Jason usually bet on the value of the Japanese yen against the pound. He said that although there were other opportunities, sticking to two currencies made him an expert. He certainly displayed an encyclopaedic knowledge of those currency movements. He bet that the Japanese currency would increase in value thanks to predicted increases in the country's exports. It was something he'd done dozens of times. Sometimes he was wrong and lost a bit, but more often he was right and made more than he lost. The currency didn't move by much, so each profit or loss was small, but it all added up. Overall, he was right more than he was wrong, and the money pile grew. But it seems Jason grew impatient and was frustrated by the trickle of profits. A few months ago we discussed how much I was investing and Jason said he wanted to increase the amount, that if I invested ten times more my profits would be ten times bigger.'

'So you gave him more money to invest?'

Mike shook his head. 'No, I...' He paused as he sat on the railing, holding on to the flagpole. 'He wanted twelve million, so I would earn a year's profit every month. But I learnt a while ago that when you take big risks, you risk losing everything. I nearly did that once in my career and I wasn't about to do it again. I told him no, we stick with just a few million. Everything was going well, and I saw no need to change. Jason asking for so much made me nervous, especially as he'd always been cautious and advocated the benefits of being steady.'

'So Jason suddenly wanted to take much bigger risks? Why the sudden change of tack?'

'That I don't know. We argued about the money. Obviously I was angry about losing it, but I was even more annoyed that he wasn't telling me everything. Why had he suddenly become so reckless? In the years I'd known him I never doubted his integrity, but something was different. He'd used leverage – basically borrowed money using my millions as security – and bet big. On top of that, he didn't buy the currency directly but bought options to buy. This is where it gets complicated and I lose myself in the technicalities, but basically he bet that the price would rise and agreed to buy millions of yen for a higher price in the future. But the government surprised everyone with a massive cut in interest rates that sent the value of the yen plunging. Because of the borrowed money and the options, I risked losing everything if it kept falling. Jason was forced to sell, crystallising the loss.'

Chapter 12

Before

W e sat facing one another in two rows, holding on to the metal railing behind us as the boat bounced gently across the surface of the water. Those of us with long hair were facing into the wind so that our hair was swept behind us.

The island in front of us loomed larger, a rocky outcrop covered with lush green foliage. Most of it was in darkness, illuminated only by the crescent moon above. We were headed towards the one bright spot in the dark, rocky mass.

As we approached, the engines idled. The boat was directed towards an opening lit with fairy lights draped around a canopy of orchids that tumbled over a wooden archway that led into the restaurant.

The boat came to a gentle halt to one side of the dining area. The maître d' helped me up the step onto the dock and guided me towards the restaurant. Behind me, Alice helped Jason up the short step, her height advantage making them appear quite an unusual couple.

The restaurant appeared to be very exclusive. The tables were few and far between and all but one of them were already full with small groups, or couples sitting together in their own private space. The lighting was low, with candles and flames creating shadows on the rocky walls. The sky was open above us between the hanging white orchids, their scent filling the air and adding to the overwhelming feeling of luxury.

We were seated on the table closest to the sea at a simply dressed table. I wanted to sit with Jason or Alice; I was feeling out of my depth amid the well-heeled clientele, underdressed and fraudulent amongst the wealth and privilege. But the seats were taken quickly and, like the last child in a game of musical chairs, I was forced to take the last one between Charlie and Mike's son, Nicholas.

As we sat, he turned towards me. 'We haven't been introduced yet. I'm Nicholas.'

I offered my hand. 'Summer. Pleased to meet you, Nick.'

'It's Nicholas, not Nick. I hate being called Nick,' he replied curtly.

I sank down into my seat a little. 'Well, it's nice to meet you, Nicholas.' I tried to keep my voice even and made a mental note to use his full name in the future. He was young, only a few years older than his sister Daisy, but with none of her easy charm.

I turned just as a handsome waiter leant over me with a menu, a single sheet of paper, with six items on it. There were no prices.

Charlie, sensing my puzzlement, leant towards me. 'These are just the starters,' he said quietly. 'If you needed to ask the price then you've come to the wrong restaurant. Don't worry, the bill is covered.'

'No. I couldn't just...'

Charlie cut me off. 'You'll have no choice tonight. Just relax

49

and enjoy the evening.'

I looked down at the menu again. Everything was in French, but I wasn't sure I'd have understood it had it been in English. I resorted to what I always did when I travelled and selected at random.

Waiters came out with bottles of pink champagne and began pouring. I wasn't sure I needed anymore champagne right now, but only Daisy was served an alternative. I poured a glass of water from one of the bottles on the table to slow myself down.

After our glasses had been filled, Mike stood up. 'It's so fantastic to have you here with us. It seems to have been an age since we've all been together, family and friends.' Nicholas shifted in his seat next to me as Mike continued. 'This year we welcome Jason, Alice and Summer. Jason has worked so hard for us over the last few years, and he's surpassed himself during this last year.'

I looked across at Jason. I expected him to be grinning widely but somehow he looked sheepish, even uncomfortable. Maybe he was more modest than I'd thought.

'So let's all raise our glasses to Jason and say thank you for all you have done,' Mike finished. We all stood and toasted Jason, while he sat with an awkward smile on his face and weakly offered his thanks.

I don't know if it was the ambiance, the champagne or warmth of the evening, but food had never tasted as divine as it did that night. Was this how the wealthy ate every day? It seemed impossible that fish – the same fish that I'd eaten so many times before – could taste so heavenly. What magic was added to transform a simple sea bass into such perfection? Every tiny dish – monkfish curry, swordfish steaks – melted on the tongue, every plate better than the last.

I looked around at my fellow diners. Only Alice had a similar look of ecstasy to mine as she ate. Had the others become immune to the power of this food? Had familiarity made the exceptional ordinary? It was hard to believe you could ever eat like this and not be overwhelmed by it.

I turned to Nicholas and tried to break the ice with him again. 'I can't get over how incredible this food is. Every mouthful triggers a massive rush of endorphins.'

'It is good here. Dad loves it – he brings us here every year.'

I was pleased that he had responded in a friendlier tone. We had to spend the next few weeks together and I really wanted to get on with everyone.

As I put down my glass, it was immediately refilled by the invisible staff who seemed to be always just out of sight. I forced myself to ignore the champagne and reached for the glass of sparkling water instead. 'Are you a cricket fan as well?'

'Cricket is Dad's thing really, but obviously I've been sucked into it after years of indoctrination. It's a bit of a religion in this family.'

I smiled at him. 'Well, there are worse sports to follow. At least it is played in the summer under blue skies. I've never really watched a match, but I've always quite liked the idea of a day in the sun with a bottle of wine, a deckchair and a picnic.'

'Quite,' replied Nicholas, seeming to lose interest in the conversation. He looked over at his dad who was deep in conversation with Alice and Jason.

Chapter 13

After

Charlie and Jane joined us, just as I was going to ask Mike when he knew things had gone wrong with the trade – and when Jason knew. Was it before he went scuba diving? Jason had seemed a little off colour at the meal on the island. Had he known then? When did he tell Mike?

Jane smiled warmly at us as she continually swatted away hair that refused to stay in place in the breeze. Mike beckoned to her to come and see the dolphins but, as we looked down, they had vanished as if disturbed by the interruption as much as I was.

Charlie and Jane talked as if Jason's death had been pre-planned, about how sad it all was but how Mike was right to carry on. Life went on, and surely Jason would have agreed. It was so easy to put words into the mouth of a dead person to suit your own agenda. Charlie turned the conversation to cricket and Mike was lured in, seemingly unable not to talk about it if the topic was raised.

Jane and I moved away a little. I wanted to ask about Beth. 'Have you spoken to Beth today?' I asked. 'It seems like ages since I've seen her, and I was getting a little worried.'

'After Jason was found, I helped her back to her cabin,' Jane replied. 'She could barely walk – her legs kept buckling under her. I helped her onto her bed and she lay motionless, staring at the ceiling, not moving, not blinking, barely breathing. I sat with her for a while, stroking her hand. Looking back, I guess we were both in shock, but Beth was really struggling. Eventually I went out and found some Jack Daniels, poured a good measure, added a dash of water and brought it in for her. I managed to get her up onto the pillows and drink it. It was before breakfast, but she didn't even flinch as I forced her to take a mouthful.'

'I guess none of us know how we might react in a situation like that. How was she when you left her?'

'I stayed with her for an hour or so, trying to comfort her. There were no tears, no wailing, just a blankness that had descended over her features.' Jane turned and looked at me square on. 'To see someone die like that is shocking. It shakes you to the core, and you aren't yourself. But when Beth came round, it was in an instant, like she'd been pumped full of adrenalin. She looked at me, screamed at me to get out and then threw the whisky tumbler as I backed towards the bedroom door. I was so taken aback that I didn't even respond. I sat down outside her bedroom and composed myself, trying to process what had just happened. I could hear muffled sobbing from behind the closed door, so I left.'

Jane was still clearly shaken by her experience with Beth, and pulled a packet of cigarettes out of a hidden pocket in her floral-print maxi dress. She flipped one cigarette up single handed and offered it to me. As I declined, she moved the pack to her mouth and pulled out the cigarette. Tucked in the packet was a thin lighter, which produced a hot plate like a car lighter rather than a flame.

'I haven't seen or heard from Beth since, but I've seen a tray taken in with food and two bottles of wine. The same tray was carried out with the food untouched and the wine bottles empty. It's not out of character for Beth, mind you – she's always drunk copious amounts. She's always the one to open the first bottle of the day and the last one at night. This feels different though, and I do worry about her. But I haven't wanted to face her again yet.'

'Mike must see her. Or whoever takes in her food.'

'I guess so, but Mike and Beth have separate rooms and have done for years. It's due to Mike's snoring apparently, not that that should be a reason to avoid sleeping with your man. As for anyone else, I doubt they go into her room. They just leave the food in the living area.'

'Should we not check on her, at least make sure she's okay?'

'She'll come out when she's good and ready, you can be sure of that.'

Chapter 14

Before

After several days slowly exploring the delights of the French Riviera, we approached the Straits of Gibraltar early in the morning. The sun was still hanging low in the sky, lighting the ocean with orange sparkles. As we sailed closer to land, the water transformed from its deep blue to a brilliant turquoise; it shimmered in the morning light. Mike and Nicholas acted as lookouts as we came into shallower water, watching below the water line for any signs of rocks.

I stood at the stern. As I looked intently at the land in the distance, Yasmin lowered the anchor and came over to talk to me. 'That's Ceuta in the distance, pronounced See-oo-ta. Not many people realise that part of Spain is actually in Africa. While they argue with the British over Gibraltar, Spain has its own rock here in Morocco.'

'So Spain actually reaches across the straits and into Africa? How big is this place?'

'Not so big, maybe thirty square kilometres, but it's still a thorn in the relationship between Morocco and Spain. Ceuta is a small city – tranquil, yet cosmopolitan. It has some unique fauna and flora thanks to its positioning here where the calm

Mediterranean Sea meets the brutal Atlantic Ocean.'

Yasmin ensured that the anchor was firmly set. She shouted orders to the crew as they moved quickly, setting everything in place. 'We need to be careful with the anchor. When two oceans meet, strong currents can be dangerous.' She walked away, leaving me looking south towards this strange part of Europe in Africa.

Just then, Alice clapped her hands. 'Okay, everyone. Mike kindly allowed us to anchor down here so that those who want to scuba dive can. I know Jason and Nicholas are keen, and I'm going to buddy up with Jane. The rest of you are free to snorkel, swim or just chill on board.'

'Alice, I didn't know you could scuba dive,' I said, surprised.

'Jason and I went to Egypt and took a diving course in the Red Sea last year. We loved it, didn't we, Jason?' Jason didn't respond but sat fiddling with the string on his shorts, tying and untying it. 'Hey Jason, are you in there?' Alice called.

Jason looked up; he seemed confused and utterly distracted.

'The diving last year. We loved diving, didn't we?' Alice persisted.

Jason was looking pale and a bit green around the gills. 'Yes, it was fab,' he replied unconvincingly. 'Although I'm not sure I'm up for it today. I might sit it out.'

'No, you can't back out. Nicholas needs a diving buddy. I'm with Jane as she is experienced, and you're with Nicholas because you're just a beginner as well. He can't go alone – he needs you with him.'

'Someone else can go instead of me.'

'Absolutely not,' Alice insisted. 'There isn't anyone to take your place. I asked Mike to stop here just for you. I told him you really wanted to get in some more dive time. I chose this spot with you in mind because there's some fantastic diving here.' Her voice rose as she made clear the decision was non-negotiable.

Nicholas wandered over and chipped in. 'I'll take good care of you, Jason. It's a magical spot that you won't want to miss. I've always wanted to dive where the two oceans meet. Let's do this.'

Jason didn't look convinced but, knowing he was beaten, nodded his head.

Chapter 15

After

'This is probably completely inappropriate, but I need a drink – and it's past midday,' Jane said. 'Wait here and I'll grab a couple of glasses.' When she returned, we headed for two sun loungers. Jane pulled one of them into the shade, removed her wide-brimmed hat and opened the bottle.

The sun was strong again today and Jane was born a redhead with a complexion best suited to grey skies. She struggled in the sun and was constantly applying sunblock to protect her pale, freckled skin. Staying outside for too long was difficult and I felt for her. It must have been as frustrating as hell to continually hide from the sun on a trip like this.

We sat and chatted as we worked our way through the bottle until I felt the time was right to slip in a question about Mike. 'So you've known Mike for many years, then?'

'I worked in the office with Mike's father after leaving college. Mike was always around, learning the ropes, working the building sites. He kept dropping in, flirting with me, making excuses to come by,' Jane said. 'I don't kid myself,' she added hastily. 'He was practising his flirting on me and was never interested in me like that. We talked a lot, though, and I looked forward to seeing him.

'Then he met Beth at some summer party, one of those big posh affairs full of beautiful people, the type of thing Mike hated even then. It was a bit of a whirlwind romance, for Mike anyway. He was besotted with her and she certainly knew how to get a man's attention. She obviously had something that Mike liked, and within three months they were married.

'During that three-month whirlwind, I hardly saw him. He stopped dropping in and, with Beth on the scene, our friendship cooled very quickly. But it wasn't long after they married that he started coming by again. He was less flirty now, mind you. He would just hang around and talk – sometimes we sat in the office long after everyone else had gone home. The friendship remained platonic obviously, and I mean that – Mike never flirted with me again.

'We carried on like that for a couple of years. Even after I met Charlie, we stayed friends. Charlie got on with Mike – their shared sports' obsession bonded them – so I saw Mike outside the office more at social events. We've stayed friends ever since. I miss our office days, but being able to come away like this and spend time with him is wonderful.'

'That sounds really lovely,' I said. 'It's always a shame when a relationship breaks up a friendship. Sometimes jealousy gets in the way and friends of the opposite sex from the past have to be renounced as a show of commitment.'

'Some people are insecure and need to do that, but Beth isn't one of those girls. She's always had Mike wrapped around her little finger. Maybe she'd have reacted differently if I'd been some hot little number, but I don't think she's ever seen me as a threat.'

Poor Jane. Unrequited love must be the worst. Years of being near the man you love and yet they are unattainable.

She seemed to read my mind. 'Not that any of that matters now. I met Charlie and he gets on great with Mike, so it's all dandy. Beth and I get on comfortably. Some people called her a gold digger when she and Mike first got together, but that's unkind. They have two beautiful kids, so it's not all bad.'

Jane seemed to ponder a moment before carrying on. Maybe it was the wine or the situation that pushed her to continue when ordinarily she wouldn't have. 'I don't normally talk about this, but Charlie and I couldn't have children even after two rounds of IVF. Daisy and Nicholas have been like niece and nephew to us. Daisy thought I was her aunt when she was young. I remember her drawing a picture of her family and she included me in it.

'I missed them terribly when they were sent away to boarding school, probably more than their mum did. Nicholas has drifted away a bit over the years, I think because he's more like his mum. But Daisy has all Mike's sweetness and light and we've stayed close. I've always felt very protective of her, more so than Nicholas. She's adorable, but naive and too trusting, much like her father. I feel like I have to look out for her, like I tried to do for her dad.'

'Do you still work for Mike?' I asked.

'No, that stopped when he sold the company. I still work for the business part-time, doing some bookkeeping and accounts. But I still give my opinion to Mike as a friend and try to guide him.

'He was always too nice a man to take over the business. His father was a sharp, ruthless businessman who never let anyone get the best of him. His deal-making was shrewd and he was constantly one step ahead of the competition, driving down costs and pushing up prices. Mike shadowed his father for years and tried to learn the trade, but his good nature made him a bad businessman. You can't be generous in business or others will take advantage of you. Look at how he's been with Jason – far too trusting and then blowing millions in a matter of hours.'

'Mike shared that with you?'

'I felt the tension before Mike said anything to me. I heard him and Beth argue and thought it was … well something else. Jason suddenly went quiet as well, but when Mike told me, it all made sense.

'Mike was too trusting again, and it's cost him dearly this time. I always thought he should be cautious where Jason was concerned. He was one of Beth's "friends", who she met on holiday. It's not a normal way to meet a financial investor, is it?'

Chapter 16

Before

I had already decided I wasn't going to dive and had got out my book so I could sketch the coastline. With only four diving suits available, it looked like I wasn't being given a choice anyway.

Daisy settled down beside me wearing impossibly trendy shades as she watched everyone get ready. With the warm waters here, full wetsuits weren't required and they slipped into jackets, adjusting, twisting and moving them around to get a good fit. Jane helped Alice with her weights, while Alice fussed and kept repeating that she would sink like a rock.

The day was perfect for diving: crisp clear skies above and only the gentlest movement in the water. As I watched them all rinse their goggles and fit them, I started to wish I'd pushed Alice harder to let me dive with them.

The girls wanted to explore a shallower area near the cliffs, while Nicholas said he wanted to explore the cliff edge where the seabed suddenly dropped away into the deep ocean. Jason remained subdued as they discussed their plans, not joining in and allowing the others to get him ready. He really hadn't been himself for a few days, not since our first day at sea before the meal. Maybe he'd been seasick and not wanted to say because he was embarrassed.

The guys moved to the stern and stepped over the handrail onto the little platform at the back of the boat. Yasmin passed them their flippers. After a limp high-five from Jason, they were ready to go. The rest of us moved to the rear to watch them step backwards into the clear waters. As they hit the water, they released hundreds of bubbles as they disappeared beneath the surface.

Jason turned to look back at us on the boat, but it was impossible to discern his expression behind the goggles and respirator. Nicholas had already headed off away from the land and towards the deeper blue waters of the shelf. Jason turned away from us and followed.

Alice and Jane quickly descended into the water and headed in the opposite direction towards the land, where the water would be shallow and warm. There the light would reach the myriad of brilliantly coloured fish, turning their scales into a light show of glittering brilliance.

I returned to my sketch book and put in my earbuds. I lay back on the sun lounger, resting my pad on my knee as I set about trying to capture the beauty of the coastline in a simple pencil drawing.

After ten minutes, Daisy tapped my arm and I took out one of my earbuds. 'It's too hot now we're not moving. Let's snorkel for a bit. They'll be ages yet.'

She was right; without the breeze generated by sailing and protected by the headland, we were in a heat trap. The sweat was running down my legs and making my sketchpad damp. 'Okay, let's do it.' I put my sketchpad under the lounger, suddenly getting excited by the thought.

We grabbed snorkels and flippers and climbed over the back of the boat, laughing as we tried to put the flippers on our sweaty feet before stepping backwards into the Mediterranean. The initial shock of cold water on baking skin soon wore off and we resurfaced at the same time, smiling under our mouthpieces. We headed for shallower waters, moving quickly across the top of the water with the help of the flippers.

I turned and looked behind us at the yacht, majestic, gleaming in the morning sun. I couldn't see anyone on board, only Yasmin at the stern. She remained vigilant, looking out for the two separate groups of divers. The jet ski had been lowered into the water and was bobbing about behind the boat.

The snorkelling was exceptional, the water as clear as an aquarium. The fish didn't disappoint with their different shapes, colours and sizes, and they seemed happy to be observed, confident in their domain. The seaweeds and grasses danced beneath us as we floated just above them, barely moving, not wanting to disturb this tranquil underwater world.

I couldn't say how long we were there, but suddenly I heard a bell ringing loudly and insistently. I lifted my head out of the water, removed my goggles and looked at the boat.

On deck, half out of their kit, were Alice and Jane. Yasmin was ringing the bell. I could see Nicholas sitting on the platform at the end of the boat, but I couldn't see Jason.

I grabbed Daisy's arm. 'Let's get back,' I said urgently. 'Something's up.'

As I arrived back at the yacht, Yasmin was on the jet ski. Standing up, she was looking ahead and below her as she followed the path Nicholas and Jason had taken earlier. There was a lot of shouting at Nicholas. Alice was shaking him, screaming in his face, 'Where is he?'

Only Beth stood, silently staring at the water, a contorted look of fear on her face.

Chapter 17

After

J ane was fiercely loyal and protective of Mike, having worked and been friends with him for many years. She didn't seem to be so keen on Beth, but who could blame her if she'd been in love with Mike all these years?

They made a strange foursome. Charlie must have known that Jane still hankered after Mike, and Beth must have seen it as well; I wasn't so sure about Mike. Was it possible that he wasn't aware of Jane's feelings?

Charlie came over and joined us. He kissed Jane tenderly as he took a seat, positioning himself in the sun. Jane picked up the sun-lotion spray and misted herself with it, even though she was in the shade. As she opened her eyes and blinked away the residue, she saw Mike was alone. She touched Charlie's knee before excusing herself. 'I just need a quick word with Mike,' she murmured.

Charlie watched her go before turning his attention to me. 'So how are you, my dear?' he asked warmly.

'To be honest, I feel dreadful,' I said. 'I didn't know Jason very well, but his death has really got to me. I'm still in shock and I just don't know what to do. Obviously I want to support Alice, but it's difficult to know how. When I was widowed, I just wanted to be alone to mourn and come to terms with it. Poor Alice is stuck here with us and has no real space for herself, while we all try and make the best of the situation.'

'I feel the same,' Charlie said. 'I'm really not sure how to deal with it. I'd only met Jason a few times, and never really got to talk to him in any depth, but he always seemed such a stable young man. Whenever I spoke to him, he always talked about the plans he had for the future. There was no hint of any inner turmoil or demons.

'The problem with men is that we cover our doubts and fears with bravado. Women are so much better at talking about their problems. I only wish I'd pressed Jason more those last few days when I could see that he was troubled. He was more than just down, and I should have spoken to him and asked if he had any suicidal thoughts.'

Charlie seemed quite despondent, and I tried to comfort him. 'You might ask a friend that, but to ask someone you barely know if they're suicidal… Not many people would do that.'

'But I knew how important it was, and I'm trained in how to spot the signs. Asking someone if they're having thoughts about harming themselves when they're not won't put those thoughts into their head. If those thoughts are there, though, it can give them a chance to speak and that can help enormously. Young men are at a particular risk. I should have said something.'

Charlie paused for a moment, before continuing. 'There is one thing that bothers me, though, and keeps playing on my mind.' He stopped again, as if deciding whether his concerns should be shared. 'They say that those under the most mental stress often change their behaviour when they've decided to take their own life. For example, they may have a feeling of euphoria because they realise that they've found a solution to their problems, or they may go around putting all their affairs in order, tidying things up, saying goodbye to friends and loved ones. I don't remember Jason's mood or behaviour changing significantly on that final day.'

I cast my mind back to that final evening. Jason had been a little different maybe, but he certainly still appeared subdued. There was no sign of a sudden lifting of his mood, not in the manner Charlie was describing. How common was this sudden change in a person's mental state after they had decided to take their life? But maybe Jason hadn't already decided on suicide at that moment, and it was a spur of the moment decision later that evening. We would never know what was going on in his head, but if a moment of elation or tidying of affairs was common, Jason didn't fit that pattern.

'I think we all share those feelings of guilt now but, when you don't know someone well, it feels inappropriate to push them if they don't want to open up. I hope you know that there was nothing you could do to help,' I said, trying to reassure Charlie that he'd done nothing wrong.

We sat together for a moment and I noticed Charlie's leg bobbing up and down, the anxiety he felt manifesting in his restless leg. I reached out and placed my hand on his arm; it was a moment when physical contact felt right. 'Everyone has taken this hard, Charlie. We're only human and it affects us all deeply. Beth seems to have taken his death particularly badly.'

'Yes, yes, she has,' remarked Charlie. 'They were close, I believe. I often watch people's body language, and Beth's always changed when Jason was around.'

'Do you know how they met?'

'Not really, only bits and pieces I heard from Jane. As I understand it, Beth would go away on her own on shopping weekends or to charity events. She had a friend she went with sometimes, but often she took off by herself, saying she enjoyed the solitude. I understand it was on one of those weekends down on the Côte, a chance meeting. She got into conversation with Jason and thought how he and Mike might get along, so she invited him to Geneva where he could meet Mike. At least, that's how Jane told it to me. I never really got the whole story, but,' Charlie lowered his voice, 'I wouldn't put it past Beth to have reeled Jason in. Jason got lucky because she was married to a millionaire. Also, as I understand it, Jason and Alice were close to broke and Jason was desperate for a well-paying client. He was a good-looking young guy, and Beth would have been easily charmed by him. I could be wrong, but Beth would have been quite a target for him.'

'You really think that's what happened? That Beth picked Jason up and used Mike's money to get his attention?'

'I don't know what was said, what are just Jane's assumptions or my suspicions. I know that Mike adores Beth, but I've never seen that affection reflected back from Beth. They have a marriage that works for them, but it doesn't appear to be all rosy to an outsider.'

I hadn't expected Charlie to reveal so much about his friends. He hardly knew me, but he was ready to share his suspicions about Beth. Jane's jealousy of Beth ran deep, and yet Charlie ignored or accepted it.

It was interesting to hear how Jane mistrusted Jason and his motives. I'd only known Jason for a short while but he'd struck me as genuine, someone who would've had Mike's interests at heart when he invested for him. He'd certainly looked desperate after realising he'd lost the money. But how well did I really know him?

Jason seemed smitten by Alice. He was a true gentleman towards her, always checking she had everything she needed, jumping up to get her a cushion or pour her a drink. The suggestion that he might have been so easily seduced by Beth seemed unlikely. I'd never seen him look at anyone else when we were in Monaco, and there'd been no shortage of distractions there. Would he really be tempted by Beth in that way? It seemed improbable.

The story of how they'd met was slightly different to the one Alice had told me. Had Jason lied to her? Alice's version was that Jason had met Mike first at a conference and then just happened to run into Beth and Mike at a motor show. I couldn't see Jason as either the seducer or the seduced. He just didn't fit the profile, unless his behaviour around Alice was all a performance...

Chapter 18

Time seemed to stand still as we watched the jet ski circle, searching for a sign of Jason. Suddenly it sped up and we all instinctively turned in the direction Yasmin was heading. There was a shape floating on the surface of the water.

Without a word, Charlie dived in the water and started swimming furiously towards it. A strange silence fell over us as we watched. Charlie reached the jet ski and helped a struggling Yasmin to remove the oxygen tank and heave the body out of the water. He laid Jason on his front across the jet ski and Yasmin began smacking and rubbing his back.

Moments passed before we saw the body jerk and a lungful of water leave Jason. On the boat, there was a collective exhalation of breath; we realised that, as one, we'd been holding our breath and fearing the worst.

Yasmin turned the jet ski and carefully steered it slowly towards us as Jason's limp body dragged in the water. As he was lifted onto the boat, he vomited and coughed up copious amounts of water. That seemed like a good thing; CPR was not required, and hopefully there would be no lasting damage.

Mike and Nicholas took one arm each and lifted Jason inside the cabin, out of the sun. They lay him on his front on a sofa so he could finish emptying his lungs. I caught Nicholas's expression as he looked down at Jason; was that a look of concern for Jason or for himself? It was hard to tell.

As Alice's fear and anger subsided, she sat beside Jason and stroked his head. She said she would sit and watch over him.

Without a word, Beth brought out a duvet and tenderly laid it over Jason, tucking the edges around him. 'Where's the nearest hospital?' she asked. For a moment the room fell silent. 'He really should get checked out by a doctor. He nearly drowned out there.'

We all looked to Mike.

'Well, we could drop you and Jason off,' he said to Alice. 'But our schedule is tight, so I'm afraid we wouldn't be able to wait. I don't think a doctor is needed, though. Do you, Alice?'

I could see her weighing up the options. On the one hand, Jason probably did need to be checked out properly by a doctor to ensure no lasting damage; on the other hand, then their dream holiday would be over – and, by extension, mine as well. 'I think Jason will be fine,' Alice said. 'His breathing is okay now. He just needs some proper rest. Let's continue.'

'Are you sure?' I asked. 'Alice, he nearly died out there.' I looked around for support, but only Daisy and Charlie nodded their heads in agreement.

'Yes, yes, he'll be fine, won't you, Jason?'

Jason said nothing but gave a small smile to acknowledge that he'd understood the conversation. It was settled; crazy as it sounded, our trip would continue.

A subdued atmosphere fell over the boat. As soon we left Jason to rest under the watchful eye of Alice, Nicholas disappeared, no doubt to hide away in his cabin. Everybody else seemed to spend the day alone, sunbathing, reading, always restless as they waited for news.

It was late in the afternoon when Alice came out to tell us that Jason had woken up and was talking. He was sitting up, feeling much better and appeared to have suffered no lasting damage. She said that we could go and see him if we wanted to. The wave of relief was evident. Mike seemed very thankful, while Beth's body sagged as if it had been held together by tension and anxiety which had suddenly evaporated.

We made our way into the lounge area. Jason was propped up, still looking a little worse for his experience, but alive and functioning again. He began to explain what had gone wrong. Nicholas appeared in the doorway just as he started to speak.

'We were diving along the underwater cliff, exploring the different environments as the temperature and the depth changed. Swimming over the cliff edge was an incredible feeling. It felt like falling over a cliff, even though there's no way to "fall" when you're under water.

'After about half an hour, at around eighteen to twenty meters down, I noticed the reading was still 130 bars. There was plenty of air left, just under half a tank. Nicholas gave me the okay signal and I responded. Everything was good. He indicated that we were going to head back, so we both turned and started to kick back the way we'd come. However, when I checked five minutes later, the reading had suddenly dropped to thirty bars, even though I'd ascended a bit and by rights I should have been using less air.

'I found myself swimming harder and harder. The current was pushing me to a standstill. I looked ahead for Nicholas but he was facing forward, kicking hard, and I couldn't keep up.

73

That's when it started to go wrong. I guess I panicked. I was struggling against the current and trying to calm my breathing down to conserve air, but the more I tried, the harder I breathed and the slower I seemed to be going.

'I wasn't sure whether to ascend and lose Nicholas or try and catch him up, so I carried on after him. I knew we'd been down for about forty minutes, so I still had at least twenty minutes to go, even with my oxygen falling fast. I remembered some of my training –at that depth I should have been using about three bars a minute of oxygen, yet I was using at least five as I tried to swim against the current. I knew the oxygen would be exhausted long before I made it back to the boat. I needed Nicholas to look back. He was still in sight, but out of reach.'

Jason looked at Nicholas standing in the doorway, but the boy was staring down at his feet and said nothing. I saw a shiver go through him. His skin looked pale and clammy, even with the heat of the afternoon.

Jason continued. 'I kicked on, trying to control my swimming and to breathe more easily and still make progress. It wasn't happening, though. I was losing touch with Nicholas. When I looked down at the seabed, I didn't seem to be moving forward at all. Panic set in and I started to imagine that I was running in quicksand, unable to move my limbs.

'I knew that the more I panicked, the faster I'd breathe and the quicker my tank would empty. When I looked at my levels, I could see that I was already into the red. I had to come up to the surface. I'd left it too late to ascend safely as I had been taught, and I would have to risk the bends. The last thing I remember was turning upwards and thrashing my legs wildly as I tried to reach the surface before my air ran dry.'

The room fell silent. From the doorway, Nicholas spoke

weakly. 'I thought you were behind me. I would never have left you on purpose.'

Chapter 19

After

The days were passing more slowly now as everyone came to terms with what had happened to Jason. Beth was still completely out of sight; Alice spent most of her time in her cabin, and Nicholas never seemed to be anywhere near me. It was quite surreal; I was surrounded by people that I didn't really know, and who I knew I would never see again in a few weeks' time.

The yacht was moving at a fair pace, a strong breeze almost lifting us out of the water as we moved westward. I spent the day with a book but found myself reading the same paragraph over and over again, my mind unable to relax and let the words in. Details were nagging me that wouldn't let go. The diving accident was probably caused by Jason's lack of focus due to his money worries – but what if him nearly drowning had not been an accident?

I decided to find Yasmin and get a few things clear in my head. She was in the chartroom at the computer with the weather forecasts on screen. 'Are we set for fair weather now?' I asked.

'Nothing to stop us for the next couple of days at least. It's about time we had some better luck. This trip is unlike anything I've ever done before. You wouldn't believe how uneventful last year's journey was!'

I took a seat opposite her as she crossed her legs and looked at me. 'So what's your take on everything that's happened. Was it a series of unfortunate events?' I asked.

Yasmin raised an eyebrow at my understatement. 'Shit happens, and sometimes it happens all at once. The bit that bothers me is that it was all connected to Jason.'

'It bothers me, too,' I said. 'I can't help thinking back to the dive accident and wondering how much of an accident it was? Did someone tamper with the air? How could Nicholas not have noticed Jason wasn't there? Could Jason have deliberately released the air to try and kill himself?'

'Well, I think you can forget that last one. Seriously – underwater suicide? How desperate would you have to be to try and kill yourself under water? I live on the water and my biggest fear is death by fire or drowning, both of which are possible. I've heard of a suspected suicide once before. It was officially put down as drowning, but the guy had attempted suicide before and some suspected that he succeeded while scuba diving. But we'll never know for sure.

'No, it looks like carelessness to me. Charlie dumped the tank and everything when he pulled Jason from the water so I can't double check the equipment, but it was in perfect working order when I checked it that morning. Could someone have tampered with it afterwards? Possibly – the gear isn't locked away. But it seems more likely that Nicholas was careless and didn't check that Jason was alright. Jason was inexperienced, and Nicholas can be a bit gung-ho. He may have gone further and deeper than he should have and not listened to my warnings about the currents and not pushing it.'

'So Jason's tank could have been tampered with?'

'Of course it's possible. A small hole in the tank or the air tube could have resulted in the air pressure falling much quicker than Jason would expect. With all the bubbles being expelled, a leak could go unnoticed.'

'Why did Charlie dump the tank and the gear?'

'We were trying to pull Jason up onto the jet ski but he weighed too much. Those tanks and weights are heavy enough when dry. We couldn't get a grip on him, so Charlie unclipped Jason's equipment. Being empty, it just sank. It wasn't our priority at the time – it all happened very quickly.'

Without the tank we were stuck. According to Yasmin, a suicide attempt was possible but unlikely. Tampering was possible but, without the gear, checking for that was a dead end.

Had Nicholas left Jason deliberately? There were certainly some unanswered questions. Nicholas was Jason's dive buddy; when you dive with someone it's for one reason only, to look out for each other to avoid situations like this. Was Nicholas careless or malicious?

'I know what you're thinking, Summer. How can this happen when you have a buddy? Well, ninety percent of divers who die every year are not alone. Things can happen when you're down there. Time moves in different ways, there are distractions and currents that can separate you. I'm not suggesting that Nicholas did nothing wrong, but it's not clear cut that the partner is to blame if a buddy gets into trouble. Although your dive partner doesn't normally have a grudge against you.'

Chapter 20

Before

We ate together most days, although it was rare that everyone was there for dinner. But after the dive incident, we all sat down together that evening. The atmosphere was much less jovial.

Mike and Beth were tense. Every time Jane smiled at something Mike said, Charlie appeared to stiffen. Nicholas seemed to have a problem with just about everyone – he'd been getting moodier by the day. Jason was quiet and thoughtful; his brush with death was obviously bothering him, but there was something else as well. To me, even Alice seemed off.

Thank goodness for Daisy. Her manner was consistently cheerful and prevented the table from falling into a solemn silence. She lifted my spirits. The trip was slipping into awkwardness for me, yet my options were limited. I was faced with these same eight faces every day for the next few weeks.

A lot of wine was always consumed; it appeared at every meal except for breakfast, although I'm sure I'd smelled some on Beth early in the morning before now. That evening, as she topped up the glasses yet again, Mike nipped in with some sarcastic comment. Even so, he didn't stop her filling his glass.

Thankfully I was not sitting near Nicholas, though I could still hear him slurring his words as he spoke to Charlie. As the main course was whisked away and the cheese board produced, along with its requisite bottle of port, he became more animated.

'So, a solid business plan in place, a billion-dollar market, all the ducks are lined up on this – and yet he won't put up a little seed money.' The table hushed, knowing who Nicholas was referring to.

'Nicholas, it's been a long day,' Mike said. 'Let's not bring this up again now.'

'What, you don't want everyone to know how you dismiss your son? How you have no faith in him? Is that it?'

'I have faith in you that if this idea is as great as you say, you'll make it work. You start small and build slowly. Someone who starts with a fortune will learn nothing. Money should never come easily, and it doesn't grow on trees. When you have it, it doesn't stick to you.'

'You mean like when you take on your dad's business, run it down for a few years and then flog it off!' Nicholas spat viciously.

'I worked for my old man for thirty years before that. I started at twelve years old. You've never had to graft a day in your whole life, what with your private schools and holiday camps.' Mike was becoming quite animated now as his voice began to rise. The rest of us seemed unsure where to look as his face reddened.

'Those were things *you* made me do! You wanted us to be educated, and sound educated, and attend private schools. Now you throw it back in my face!'

'My education was in the business and I wanted more for

80

you,' Mike retorted. Beth put a hand on his arm, but he brushed it off. 'My dad never saw any value in school and wanted me in the business as early as possible. I learnt how to run it, but that never made me a great businessman – I know that, and I can admit it. You can be better than that, thanks to your brains and your schooling. If you believe in your idea, you'll find outside investors or a way to make it work. Even if I wanted to chuck a load of money at it, I couldn't right now.'

Nicholas turned his gaze towards Jason and snarled, 'Well, we know why that is,' before sliding out his chair and getting unsteadily to his feet. He went to say something else but stopped himself before stomping off towards his cabin, holding on to the wall as he went.

Chapter 21

After

As reading seemed beyond me, I decided to sunbathe and listen to a little music. At moments like these, staying awake was always a problem. The warm air and the motion of the boat seemed to lull me into a doze at any hour of the day. Daisy managed to rouse me, though, by pulling out one of my earbuds and asking me what I was listening to.

'Hi, you,' I replied. 'Just some chilled sounds from the eighties. Here, have a listen.'

She pulled up a lounger and listened in, both of us enjoying Prince singing about purple rain. 'Don't know that, but it sounds okay,' she said as she handed me back the earbud.

I took out the other one and put my music to one side. Now Daisy was here, the peace was surely broken.

'Do I need to lose weight?' she asked earnestly. 'I do, don't I? You'll be honest, I know.'

'What made you say that, Daisy? You have a beautiful figure for a girl your age and you certainly shouldn't be worrying about it.'

'Under a photo of me on Facebook, somebody's written "Daisy Donuts on vacation".'

'Really? Well, that it isn't a friend of yours because it's not only cruel, it's also untrue. You need to ignore those comments.' It really annoyed me how girls seemed to take pleasure in pulling each other down, bitching and judging based on how someone looked in a photo.

This obsession with a perfect body, whatever that was, had always angered me. Like Daisy, I wasn't super skinny: I was what people used to call normal. Some might advise me to tone up around the middle a bit, which I was sure I'd do someday, but at that moment I was quite happy with my shape.

'It's all about having self-confidence, Daisy. As you grow up, others will try and tell you how to look, how to dress, what makeup to wear. Don't listen to them. You're beautiful. You just need to tell them that you love the way you look, so you won't be changing it for anyone else.'

'Yeah, you're right. She's not nice. I just wish everyone would be kinder.'

'How are you feeling about Jason?' I asked.

'I don't know really. I think I'm alright and then I just start crying for no reason.'

'Have you told anyone how you feel? Your mum or dad?'

'I haven't seen Mummy – she wouldn't answer the door to me. Daddy hugged me, but I know how angry he was with Jason, so I don't think he understands why I'm so upset.' Daisy started to cry and wiped her eyes on the beach towel. I reached out and hugged and we were both in tears for a moment.

As she gradually stopped crying, she lay back on the lounger. 'I wish we were skiing instead of this. There is nothing to take my mind off it on this boat, nothing to do except watch the water go by and wait for the next meal. I'm bored with sunbathing.'

'I've never been skiing so I can't compare it, but I think you're right. There's only so much lying about that you can do.'

Daisy laughed, thinking I was joking. 'Everyone goes skiing once a year. What did you do in the winter when you were my age?'

'Good question. What *did* I do? Lots of hanging around with my friends and lots of studying – I don't know really. But certainly not skiing! We could never have afforded a ski holiday.' Daisy was clearly well-travelled for a girl of her age, but she was so naive. In her world everyone went skiing, everyone had a yacht and an extensive wardrobe full of everything a teenage girl could want. Would she ever escape that bubble and see the real world, the world Alice and I grew up in, where you had to fight to avoid a life of soul-destroying work and you had little control over your future? Probably not, and maybe she would never need to. Even now, with all the money Jason had lost, I doubted anything would change her lifestyle.

Beth's absence was still bothering me. Nobody seemed to have seen her for days. 'Have you seen your mum today, Daisy?' I asked.

'Daddy says she's sick. She picked something up in Morocco and we have to leave her alone in case it's contagious.' Daisy nervously twirled and twisted her long blonde hair around her fingers as she answered, as if she knew she was repeating a lie.

She talked and I listened. Her infectious youthfulness took my mind of Jason, and our conversation seemed to help her forget what had happened for a while. We talked about schools and girlfriends, and she asked me about my school days with Alice. Daisy would never go to a college like mine or mix with the type of kids I did, and somehow I pitied her for that. I

84

could no more imagine an expensive private college life in Switzerland than she could picture life in an inner-city college, but I had a feeling her schooling would offer a less fulfilling experience, even if she did come away with a smattering of Latin.

'So are you going to the same college as Nicholas went to?'

'No, of course not. Nicholas was at a boy's college where he studied business so he could become this amazing businessman and take over the world.' She said it without sarcasm. She wasn't belittling her older brother; she was too sweet for that.

'Yes, I heard him talk about some business that he wants to start when we get back.'

'Well, maybe not straight away. He wanted Daddy to give him the money to start it up. He got very angry with Daddy and Jason when he was told no.'

I remembered the dinner when Nicholas had stormed out, and how much of his anger had seemed to be directed at Jason for some reason. 'Why would Jason stop your dad investing in Nicholas? Surely Jason wouldn't have anything to do with it.'

'I don't know, but when I was crying yesterday about Jason, Nicholas came into my cabin and started on at me. He wanted to know why I was crying over Jason. He said he was a crook and a fraudster who'd lost us our inheritance. He said Jason had blown his chance of building an amazing business. I told him to leave me alone and stop being so nasty about Jason, but he laughed at me. He told me I was stupid for shedding tears over someone who'd taken away our entire future.'

I hadn't got the feeling that Mike would ever hand over the money to Nicholas, bearing in mind what he'd said during their row. And having just lost millions, Mike would be more cautious than ever. I didn't know how much of Mike's fortune

Jason had lost but, whatever the amount, it must have left him feeling a less secure about investing in anything. If Nicholas did really blame Jason for the loss of his dream, though, was it reason enough for Nicholas to kill him?

'Your brother is a hard guy to talk to,' I said slowly. 'He doesn't seem to like me, and he comes across as wound up and angry all the time. Is he always like that?'

'He can be a real brat, and he often doesn't get on with Daddy these days, but he's normally better than this. He is awkward sometimes – he thinks being mean and moody is somehow cool, and he'll get what he wants by being less rather than more charming. I think he likes you okay,' she added. 'But he's never been able to talk to girls, and he hasn't got any better as he's gotten older.'

Daisy surprised me with her attempt to be insightful; it wasn't what I'd come to expect from her. However, in this case I thought she was wrong. Her brother had had a chip on his shoulder during the whole trip. Some guys are shy and awkward with women, but Nicholas seemed to have gone out of his way to be rude and sullen with me. That was way beyond simple bashfulness.

If Daisy was right and this was out of character, what had caused the sudden change? Nicholas seemed to have a problem with Jason and was always around when Jason had his 'accidents'. None of that proved him guilty, but it did make him look pretty suspicious.

Chapter 22

Before

After Nicholas stormed off from the meal, the table fell quite for a moment. No one wanted to be the first to break the silence. At the same time, I noticed that my untouched glass of port was sloshing around, threatening to spill over the sides; the sea was becoming rougher.

Just as the silence threatened to become awkward, a wave hit and two glasses fell sending blood-red port across the table. Jane jumped up, just too late to avoid being covered.

At that moment, Yasmin appeared. 'Sorry, Mike. This is going to get rougher than forecast, so we're going to have to get all this stored away. Could I have a hand locking down? We need to get both sails down and the ship secured, and I am shorthanded on deck.'

As if to reinforce the urgency of her tone, another wave hit the yacht and she lurched to one side before correcting herself. Cutlery and glasses – anything that wasn't secured in place to the non-slip mat that covered the table – were sent flying.

That second wave sobered everyone up and we all leapt into action. I was pleased I'd spent time with Yasmin learning how the sails and rigging worked, and volunteered to help her.

None of us were dressed for locking down a yacht in a storm, but we grabbed heavy waterproof coats and dashed up onto the deck. Although normally the sun would have been close to setting by now, this evening the sky was almost totally black. No light escaped through the clouds. Looking out from the yacht gave the impression of looking into nothingness. Only the brilliance of the masthead light, situated over the fore and aft centreline, allowed us to see the white crests of the waves that were building up. Without that, we wouldn't have been able to see what was coming until it hit us.

As the waves crashed in, we knew that the sudden nature of the squall had put us in real danger. We took our orders from Yasmin. Obviously she planned to sail us through this storm rather than lying ahull and riding it out.

Alice was sent to take over from the autopilot at the helm and to steer us as best she could to avoid being side on to the waves and risk being rolled. Charlie and I were tasked with reefing the smaller foresail, while the others tackled the mainsail. In theory I'd learned reefing all those years ago with Alice, but I'd never had to put it into practice like this.

We worked quickly together to lower the sail and secured the reef tack to make it smaller; that would hopefully prevent the wind ripping the sail off or, even worse, dragging the boat and capsizing us. As the ocean continued its relentless pitching and pounding, we worked to fix the sail in place.

As we satisfied ourselves that it was secure, I looked around to check on the progress of the mainsail. With the foremast now reefed, the mainsail was taking the full force of the gusts. I could see Jason struggling to pull on his line; the after-effects of the dive and the weight of the wind in the sail were making him struggle to wind it in, as the sea threatened to throw him across the deck.

Rain as well as sea spray had started to lash at us now, leaving the deck slippery underfoot. Charlie pulled my arm and shouted above the sound of the noise of the wind to help him lock things down at the bow. We made our way tentatively to the front as if we were walking on the back of a bucking bronco. Once there, we tightened the storage boxes that held the sun loungers and parasols.

The yacht suddenly lurched upwards, turning ninety degrees. We both grabbed at the handrail, gripping until the metal started to cut into us. Although the waves were not breaking, their height sent shivers through me. Having only sailed on calm waters in nothing more than a shower, this was not something I'd ever imagined experiencing.

We found ourselves facing an enormous wave whipped up by the wind. It dwarfed the yacht, rising up and up in slow motion before we slammed into it, then crashing over us and threatening to drag us from the rail. Time slowed down as I held on. I could no longer see Charlie; I could no longer see anything beyond darkness.

As the yacht righted itself and the wave receded, I shouted to Charlie that we had to get inside before we were hit again. We ran for the patio door.

Once inside, the drop in noise was noticeable. The roar from the wind and the ocean was now muffled, replaced by the sound of the rain slashing and ripping at the windows. Charlie and I shook off our coats and hurried through to see how everyone else was doing.

The dining room was cleared; everything that could be fixed in place had been secured. Just then the hatch to the stern burst open. Mike and Yasmin came tumbling in, carrying somebody between them, followed by a concerned looking Alice and Jane.

'Quickly, get me the first-aid kit from the galley,' Yasmin shouted.

I realised it was Jason they were carrying – and blood was covering his face.

Beth gasped when saw him she and rushed forward to help.

'Jason again! What is happening here?' said Daisy, as they removed Jason's waterproof and lay him on the sofa.

As the first-aid kit was brought to her, Yasmin set about cleaning the blood away to reveal a gaping wound on the back of Jason's head. 'It's going to need some stitches,' she said tersely. 'It's deep and he's concussed. I'll stitch him up. Alice, you stay here and help me check him over. Mike, can you take everyone along to the lounge while we wait this storm out? Stay away from windows and stay seated. It's going to take a while.'

We headed off, leaving Yasmin and Alice to tend to Jason. I was filled with a mixture of shock at what had happened to Jason together with fear for us all; the squall didn't seem to be abating and, if anything, the rain was falling harder.

We went to our rooms to dry off before meeting up in the lounge. We sat at a distance from one another, listening to the storm, everyone deep in thought. Even Daisy had been silenced by what was happening. Then Beth got up, grabbed an unopened bottle of wine and started to fill a mug with it. She didn't bother to offer it around.

The main patio door slid open, and Nicholas's soaking-wet head appeared. What was he doing out there? I'd thought he was sobering up in his room.

'Where's Yasmin?' he demanded. 'The mainsail has ripped, and we need to get it down. Lotte and Martina are struggling because of the gusts and we need Yasmin.'

Jane ran off to find Yasmin. Charlie and I dragged on our wet things again, ready to face the squall one more time.

Chapter 23

After

There was a limit to how long I could lay around sunbathing and I was now well past it. I needed to do something, but my options were limited. The yacht had Yasmin as the captain and three crew members who did practically everything for us. Even though this world was alien to me, I had to admit I'd taken to having my bed made, my breakfast prepared and my drinks brought over. But I had to find something to occupy my time. Learning navigation seemed like an interesting option, so I headed off to find Yasmin.

She stood at the helm, cup of coffee in one hand and wheel in the other, looking at the vast emptiness before her. I watched her for a few moments as she swung the wheel one way and then another in seemingly random movements. In front of her was a glass bowl containing a needle that constantly shifted a few degrees as she steered the boat.

'Hi, Yasmin, how are we doing?' I asked. 'Making up time?'

'We're winning at the moment with this breeze.'

We stood without speaking as I watched her deft movements to keep our course steadily westward. 'So, do you or one of the crew steer us all the time?' I asked.

'Mike sails, so he spends a fair bit of time up here, as does Alice, who is quite the sailor. But to be honest, the autopilot does much of the work. Mike knows what he's doing – he could do this trip without me – but he still likes the reassurance of a qualified captain and so does the insurance company. The others have had a turn. I've been waiting for you to ask. I thought you might have come up before now.'

'I didn't want to get in anyone's way, I guess,' I said, although it hadn't occurred to me that I'd be given a chance to pilot. 'If we're equipped with autopilot, why steer at all?'

'We steer because we love the feel of the boat responding to us as we tack in and out of the wind. This is the sailing bit we all love. The rest is just being a passenger.'

'But in theory, you could leave it to the autopilot if you wanted?'

'To a point, yes. We have to be aware of shipping lanes and be on the lookout for other vessels, but we're equipped with radar for that. Also whales are a risk out here. But generally, yes. I can set the autopilot to follow a course I've plotted or track a wind direction. If the sails are set correctly and the boat is balanced, we'll stay on a fairly constant course unless the wind suddenly shifts.'

I looked at the wheel and watched as Yasmin moved it slightly to make a minor adjustment. 'So does the autopilot turn the wheel for you?'

'It would on a smaller yacht, but for us the controller is connected directly to hydraulics to move the tiller. Would you like to have a go on the helm?'

'I'd love to, if you can give me some pointers.'

'Take the wheel and I'll talk you through the basics.'

Yasmin moved back. Holding the wheel required more concentration than I'd anticipated as it bounced around in my hand. I gripped it tightly with both hands and tried to hold the boat straight.

'Autopilot is off and we're sailing manually,' Yasmin explained. 'Autopilot will get us where we want to go but sailing manually will get us there quicker. The needle on the compass in front of you needs to stay west. It will bounce around, but as you adjust the wheel we'll stay on the right path. The skill, though, is to use the wind and feel the yaw – that's the roll and pitch – to keep the ride smooth while still getting us where we want to go. Modern autopilot is great for keeping us moving in the right direction and keeping the ride smooth, but it can't work the wind for speed.'

I tried to remember back to my time sailing but failed to translate what I'd learnt on a lake to what I was being asked to do here. As the needle spun towards north, I steered us back – but oversteered and left us heading south. I was constantly turning the wheel to try and find the right balance. Yasmin was patient with me, not jumping in to correct me, and I slowly learnt how to correct us.

'So in that storm Alice must have really struggled to keep us upright and moving forward.' I said, when I felt it was safe to relax my concentration a little.

'Alice did a great job in very challenging conditions. I blame myself for not predicting the severity of the storm.'

'Like you said, these things can grow without warning. And we all know how unpredictable weather forecasts can be,' I said sympathetically.

'Jason could have died…' Yasmin stopped herself finishing the sentence. 'Sorry, that was thoughtless. Jason's death seems unreal, especially after what had happened to him on the dive and then during the storm.'

I glanced quickly at her. For a moment, she looked sad. Then I said, 'That night, during the storm, Jason took quite a blow to the back of the head. I know there was a lot going on, but it bugs me not knowing how it happened.' I looked again at Yasmin.

She stared deep into my eyes, assessing me, reading my mind. 'You're wondering if someone might have hit him, aren't you?'

I hesitated a moment before responding. 'Yes. Yes, I have wondered if someone could have hit him – accidentally, I mean.'

Yasmin grabbed the wheel and pulled it down hard towards her, bringing us back on the path that I'd failed to notice I had wandered from.

'If someone hit him accidentally and knew about it, they'd have shouted for help. They didn't. I found him. If he'd been there five minutes longer, he would probably have been washed over the side. The alternative is someone deliberately hit him.' She paused as if saying it out loud had made it more conceivable. 'Almost everyone seemed to be on the deck that evening and we couldn't see much because of the weather conditions. I didn't have sight of Jason, so I can't say what happened – but anything was possible.'

As I stood there, wheel in hand, trying to keep the needle in line like some computer game, I thought about who couldn't have been near Jason when it happened. The only two people I could eliminate were Charlie and myself; everyone else could have been on the deck when Jason was struck.

'I went over to see if Jason had finished tying down,' Yasmin continued. 'We'd just been over another large wave and I saw something sliding towards the guard rail. I couldn't tell who it was at that point. I assumed the wave had knocked them off their feet and went to help them up. I only realised it was Jason when I turned him over and shone my torch at him. There was watery pink blood covering his face and his hair sticky with it. I shouted for help, but my voice was probably inaudible over the noise. Then Mike arrived, followed by Alice.'

'You didn't see Nicholas anywhere?'

'Nicholas? No. It was quite wild out there – visibility was awful. He could have been there and I wouldn't have seen him even if I'd been looking. But no, only Mike and Alice came when I shouted.'

'What about the injury. Was there anything obvious nearby that could have caused the wound?'

'Even the best-built yachts have some rough edges that could cause that type of damage.'

Yasmin doubted an accident but, frustratingly, there was no evidence one way or another. If Jason had been hit from behind in the middle of a storm, he would have known nothing about it. Apart from Charlie, I hadn't really narrowed down who could have hit Jason. Those who were angry, hurt or jealous of him seemed to include almost everyone on the boat. He had seemed like Mr Wonderful when we'd started out in Monaco, but in two short weeks he'd managed to alienate or upset everyone on board.

It was hard to believe that Jason had an awful run of bad luck and then took his own life. I'd always loved statistics – and the probability of murder was now too high to ignore.

Chapter 24

Before

The worst of the squall passed over us relatively quickly, but the sea didn't want to quieten down and kept us all unsettled. No one really slept. I sat up with Alice to watch over Jason, both of us napping when our eyes stung too much to keep them open any longer.

When Alice's room filled with brilliant sunlight, I went in search of coffee for us both. Everyone else was up and asking for news about Jason, but I had little to offer. He'd come round in the night and spoken briefly, but quickly went back to sleep, knocked out by something Yasmin had given him.

As we stood around the kitchen helping ourselves to tea and coffee, Yasmin, who had clearly been up all night, came into the kitchen. 'The good news is we survived the night. I'm sorry it wasn't as comfortable as it should have been. With the mainsail ripped, we'd no choice but to lie ahull, basically sit with the sails down. It's not normally the best tactic because we had no control and had to roll with the waves, but we avoided being swamped.

'Now for the bad news. We have no mainsail, and it can't be repaired at sea. By lying ahull, we've drifted about thirty miles off course. We have fuel, but not enough to get us the rest of the way, so we have no choice but to turn around and head back to port for repairs. We'll lose a day getting there, followed by another day or two for repairs, but to continue with just the foremast would be foolhardy and slower in the long run.

'On the plus side, we can get Jason seen by a proper doctor. If we set off now for Morocco, we can be in the port town of Essaouira in time for dinner on dry land. I've phoned ahead and they have the parts we need.'

As Yasmin spoke, Mike held his head in his hands and rubbed his temples. When she finished, he looked around the room, clearly angry. 'There are a few things I need to know. Yasmin, tell me, how did we end up in a massive fucking storm to begin with? Surely we have radar and forecasts to avoid this type of thing? Secondly, how the hell did the mast get ripped so easily after all the money I spend on maintenance? And can anyone tell me how Jason nearly ended up dead for a second time in a day?'

Yasmin shifted uneasily. 'It wasn't a storm as such that did the damage, but a squall. Those squally winds and heavy sudden rainfall are hard to predict. At this time of the year, as the temperature rises, a squall can form seemingly out of nowhere. Last night's was particularly bad, with gusts of sixty knots recorded on the anemometer. I didn't expect it, and I couldn't do much to avoid it once it was upon us. Although the worst of the gusts only last for a few minutes, it's the ferocity of the wind for those minutes that do the damage.

'Jason was helping to reef the mainsail. Conditions were so bad that we were working blind. Visibility was low, so I couldn't see him. I was just about done when I saw someone was down and darted over to help. Getting him in was the priority. It looks to me as if the line Jason was tying came loose. I've no idea how he was hit in the head, though – there's nothing obvious that could have struck him. The rip in the sail was just bad luck.'

Mike looked around the room. 'So nobody knows what happened to Jason, how he came to be unconscious with a head wound?' We remained silent. After several moments he went on, 'Well, let's see if we can get to Morocco without further incident and get this boat sorted as soon as possible, for fuck's sake! Our schedule is now very tight if I'm going to make the first test match – where, I might remind you, I'm supposed to be at the party the night before the series begins.'

He stood up and marched off towards his cabin, leaving us all feeling like naughty children. I felt especially sorry for Yasmin. She really couldn't be blamed for a broken mast during a storm, yet somehow she seemed to have received the full force of Mike's displeasure.

The atmosphere had changed. It no longer felt like I was enjoying a spectacular luxury holiday but rather enduring a trip in a confined space with a group of people I hardly knew, people I wouldn't normally want to spend a day with, let alone a month. Even Alice had become a stranger recently; even before the diving accident she'd seemed to not be herself. Her smile and sense of fun were strained, forced; she wasn't the carefree, joyous old friend she'd been back in Monte Carlo. Whatever had got to Jason had got to Alice, and she hadn't felt like sharing it with me.

I felt out of the loop, with tensions and strains all around me and no idea where they were coming from. Today was going to be tough. Without the mainsail, we would be travelling only with the motor, making painfully slow progress to Morocco.

It was a day to keep my head down, put my sunglasses on and snooze on a sun lounger. Hopefully when I woke Morocco would be in view.

Essaouira appeared just as the sun lay low in the sky and cast its orange light onto the ramparts that surrounded the city. The wind blew strongly again as we approached the harbour. I could see wind- and kite- surfers just off the sheltered beach, racing and bouncing across the gentle waves that were rolling in constantly. On top of the fortress, tourists were enjoying a breezy view across the Atlantic Ocean as towering waves crashed onto the rocks below.

We travelled south, well away from the rocks, towards the port entrance where fishing boats in their hundreds were in dock for the evening. Hordes of seagulls sat on every available perch to get the best view of any unprotected fish.

This port was so unlike the one we'd left in Monaco with its multimillion-dollar playthings for the wealthy. There were dozens of small fishing boats, all painted blue because, apparently, sardines are particularly attracted to blue and so the colour helps the fishermen in their work.

Yasmin brought us up outside a boatyard, our presence a stark contrast to the small fishing boats and the larger trawlers alongside them. As she and the crew secured us to the dock, the rest of us congregated on deck to make plans. Alice and Jane were going to take Jason to a doctor while the rest of us had an hour to explore the city before meeting to eat together in one of the seafood restaurants in the square.

We stepped onto dry land for the first time in more than a week. The sensation was unsettling; the solid ground swayed and seemed to move more under my feet than it had done at sea.

I headed off along the pier with Daisy through an incredible fish market, every stall stocked with the most amazing array of fish I'd ever seen. They looked different here; there were exotic varieties that were new to me, from small sardines right up to long eel-like creatures with ferocious-looking teeth. Also, I wasn't used to seeing them so fresh, plucked straight from the sea.

As we left the waterside market and climbed the steps onto the fortress walls, I stopped to take in my surroundings. This was my first time in North Africa, and it wasn't what I'd expected at all. The wind, beautifully named *alizee*, blew through my hair as I looked below me to the town with its blend of Moorish and European influenced architecture.

Daisy and I strolled along the seawall and explored the shops and stalls along spice-scented lanes. My land legs had finally returned and my stomach had settled and was starting to demand food. We headed south through the medina, back towards the main square where we hoped to find the others. Outside the restaurants leading to the square, acrobats entertained the diners with energetic backflips off each other's shoulders.

We found Beth, Mike, Charlie and Jane sitting outside a restaurant by the main gates to the medina just before the square. A waiter made two more place settings for us as we joined them. Daisy started to tell them about the city and what we'd seen, while Beth showed off her purchase – a flowing, yellow, robe-like dress, decorated with intricate embroidery. She seemed especially cheerful, maybe because she'd managed to find one of the only restaurants in the city that served alcohol and was already on her second glass of wine.

Mike told us that he'd booked us all rooms in a hotel just

across the square. 'We could have stayed aboard, but I think we could all do with having our feet on ground that doesn't move for a night. It's not luxurious, but at short notice it has rooms for us all. Our bags are being brought over and we are all checked in,' he said as he passed around room keys.

Jason arrived with Alice, looking remarkably well except for the cartoon-style turban bandage on his head. Everyone jumped up and fussed over him, firing questions about how he felt, should he be up and about, did he want to lie down. His smile was strained, but he reassured us and took a seat at the end of the table in the shade.

As Alice related the experience of getting Jason patched up, we ordered food. There was no question that I'd be ordering fish; I wanted to sample everything but settled for a swordfish steak. Its flesh was so delicate, it literally dissolved in my mouth. It seemed that here in Essaouira you didn't need to be a millionaire to find amazing food.

The conversation around the table was relaxed. Even Mike seemed to have calmed down about the delay; at one point he stood and applauded the acrobats as they continued their seemingly endless display of strength and agility.

As a round of coffee and mint teas were served, Beth pulled out her packet of cigarettes, excused herself and wandered towards the fortress walls fronting the ocean. A few minutes later, Jason said he needed to clear his head. Alice tried to talk him out of it and insisted that she'd go with him, but he promised he'd be fine and wouldn't go far. Alice watched as he walked off through the crowds in the same direction as Beth and disappeared amongst the tourists .

I indulged in my favourite pastime of people watching as I sat enjoying mint tea that was served in a silver teapot. There were tourists from all over Europe, their accents and languages mingling as they crossed the square looking at the restaurant menus. As I sat watching, working out back stories for some of the passers-by, I saw what looked like Beth hurrying towards the hotel across the square where we were due to spend the night. She was a fair distance away, but it looked as if she were crying.

Chapter 25

After

The corridor along which our cabins were located was always dark, the mahogany-coloured wood absorbing all of the light. I slowed down and listened as I passed Beth and Mike's cabin. Engine noises drowned out most sound and solid doors blocked the rest, which made listening at the door futile.

I knocked on Jane's door and waited. A moment passed. Just as I was about to give up, the door opened a crack and she appeared, her red hair dripping onto the fluffy white towel that she'd wrapped around herself. Her skin was pink from having just stepped out of a hot shower.

'I'm sorry, Jane, I caught you at a bad time,' I said. 'I just wondered if you fancied a game of backgammon. I saw you playing with Beth before, and I haven't played for ages.'

'Yes, that would be lovely,' she replied. 'Give me five minutes to throw on a dress and I'll meet you up under the canopy.'

'Great. I'll get us some lemonade and meet you there.'

Jane closed the door and I headed for the kitchen in search of drinks. The galley was large, spacious and chic, dominated by expensive chrome fittings. Light was falling through the wide oval window above the sink. In the centre of the room was an island, chrome again, with a glass-covered preparation area. Standing there was a small, wiry man, his black hair neatly pulled back in a ponytail. He was expertly slicing carrots into a bowl.

He looked up, saw me and smiled. Like all of the staff, he was exceptionally well presented in his starched white outfit. 'Is there anything I can help you with, madam?' he asked in a heavy French accent.

'I was hoping to get some of that delicious lemonade I had yesterday – but don't worry if you don't have any.'

'Lemonade must be fresh. If you can wait two minutes, I will make some for you.'

'No, no, I don't want to trouble you if you're busy,' I protested, but it was too late: he'd already moved the carrots to one side and was chopping fresh lemons. He threw the chunks into a food mixer, poured in sugar, chilled water and ice. Within two minutes, he was sieving the mixture into a jug.

'If you need any more, just let me know. It is no trouble,' he said.

I thanked him profusely as I left the galley and went back up the stairs. I was still struggling with the idea of having staff who were there to do my bidding, although it might be something that I could get used to.

I stepped onto the deck where Jane was already sitting under the canopy with her backgammon set in front of her. 'Lemonade. Just the ticket today. It's time my liver had a rest,' she said.

'I've been thinking the same. I've never drunk as much as I have on this trip.' I poured out two glasses as we set up the backgammon board. I let Jane roll the dice first. We played quietly for a few minutes while I desperately tried to remember the rules and, more importantly, the tactics.

Finally I said, 'Nicholas talked to me after lunch today. It's the first time I've really spoken to him on this trip.'

'That doesn't surprise me,' Jane said. 'He can be very shy but he's also an arse. I saw him put on his aloof persona with you to cover his shyness. He believes he's being cool and laid back, but he just appears rude.'

'You're right. That's exactly how he came across.'

'He's like a schoolboy. He thinks that if he's obnoxious, the girl will believe he's mysterious and try harder with him.'

'That would never have worked with me,' I laughed. 'My type is smart, charming and mature, and Nicholas seems to lack all three of those qualities.'

Nicholas was a few years younger than me and he might improve as he matured, but the damage of an all-boys' school was already done. Whoever first believed that removing young boys from female company would produce a well-balanced young man who was prepared for life in the adult world? It annoyed me that nearly every British prime minister had gone to a single sex school. Was it any wonder gender equality was such a battle when most of our elected leaders didn't know how to interact with the opposite sex when they left school?

'Nicholas has decided that he doesn't need to try in life, things just come his way. He's always got his own way with Beth – he's very much a mummy's boy. He's always been her favourite. That's why he took an instant dislike to Jason – Jason seemed to challenge him for his mother's affection' Jane noticed my raised eyebrows. 'Not in the way you're thinking. I doubt Nicholas ever suspected anything untoward between them.'

Nicholas might not have done but I suspected that Jane did.

I decided to push her a little more directly. 'I heard that Beth and Jason met in the South of France, while Beth was there alone shopping and Jason was at a conference. How do you suppose they came across each other?'

Jane rolled a six and a two and started moving her pieces around the board, blocking me in the process. She hadn't been coy with me about Nicholas, but Beth was a different matter; with her loyalty to Mike, I knew I'd have to tread carefully. But I had a feeling that Jane might be one for a bit of gossip.

'When I first heard about it, I assumed Beth had targeted this handsome younger man. It wouldn't have been the first time. She can be a bit of a cougar, and she has a way of taking her pick amongst men half her age. But I'm not so sure it was all her this time. I overheard a conversation once, shortly after I met Jason for the first time, and Beth said Jason was simply a business associate. She was clearly upset with him about something, and he was trying to placate her and not cause a scene. I heard her say, "You started this, you followed me to the cafe. I spotted you earlier in the hotel lobby. You wanted this too, so don't pretend now that you didn't."'

'Did you hear what Jason said?'

'No, not really. His voice was calmer. I only heard snippets after that because Beth calmed down, but the gist of it was clear. She believed she'd been pursued. Jason had his eye on her from the start. While Beth was probably open to letting it happen, it was Jason who instigated it.'

I still found this hard to believe. That Jason was devoted to Alice had been evident all holiday; could he be the type to lead a double life, playing the devoted husband at home while playing the field outside? It seemed unlikely, but how could I know for sure?

When I thought back, maybe it was more than devotion to Alice on his part. She always expected her man to behave in a certain way; she was quite old fashioned in many of her views about how a man should treat a woman. It was more than equality with Alice; she thought men should worship at a woman's feet.

Little things she'd said in the past came back to me and reminded me how much she sounded like a country-and-western song, yearning for a time when men were gentlemen who would lay down their coat across a puddle for you to cross. Jason certainly adored Alice, but I wondered how much of his behaviour towards her was natural and spontaneous and how much he acted that way because it was expected.

'Do you think Jason could have targeted Beth because he liked older attractive women?' I asked.

'Beth is still attractive for a middle-aged woman, and she carries an air of sexuality about her, but she's not exactly to die for, is she? Jason is good looking, charming, smart – he could have had his pick of women. Would he choose someone twenty years older? No, I think Jason knew who she was and it wasn't a chance meeting. He targeted Beth because of Mike, used her to get close to Mike. He probably strung her along the whole time.'

It was a different take on the story to the one Charlie had shared. Had Jane not told Charlie everything, or were assumptions being made? I thought back to that first night in Essaouira, when I'd seen Beth hurrying into the hotel in tears. I was sure Jason had gone to talk to her and must have said something to upset her.

'Is Beth the emotional type, prone to crying easily?'

Jane stifled a smile, 'Beth is often called many things, but emotional isn't one of them.'

I picked up the dice and rolled them. Jane refilled her glass with lemonade and greedily drank the glass down in one go. We played in silence for some time while I pondered how direct to be. 'Do you think Mike suspected anything was going on between Jason and Beth?'

Jane swept her hair back away from the corner of her mouth. 'Mike has always thought Beth is perfect in every way. You could wave photos in front of his face and he'd refuse to believe them. It's not that he's stupid, but he's always been blinded by love when it comes to her. He'd do pretty much anything to protect her.'

I'd been pondering the whole Beth and Jason meeting bit. It seemed improbable to me that Jason would have been out chasing women. Beth targeting Jason seemed more likely, but it still meant that Jason allowed himself to be seduced. There was another option, though.

I had been friends with Alice through college and only kept in loose contact with her over the years, but I knew she'd always been driven by money. She desired a better life, as we all do, but was determined that she would achieve it one way or another. Could Alice have pushed Jason into chasing the big money, even subconsciously, by continually reminding him about how she wanted better, bigger house, an expensive car, another holiday? Would that not have had an effect? Could Alice even have planned it with Jason as a way to solve their money issues – befriend the wealthy wife to get to Mike?

If she had, it had worked a treat. It gave Jason an in with Mike that was very profitable for all of them until recently. Would Alice turn a blind eye while her husband flirted with another man's wife? I couldn't answer that but, if she had, how she must now be regretting ever getting involved with Mike and Beth.

Chapter 26

Before

The hotel was clean and comfortable, one of those places that blends the West with something more exotic so tourists feel they are immersed in a foreign culture, but with the reassurance of a breakfast buffet and rooms with CNN on the television.

I woke early, just as the sun was rising, and walked down to the fish market. It was already frantic with activity as boats returned with their night's catch and market traders haggled for the best boxes. I wandered, camera in hand, trying to capture that perfect shot that encapsulated all of the sights, sounds and aromas of the place.

I continued down to the boatyard where we'd moored the night before. The ripped sail was already lying on the dock. It really hadn't been Jason's day, what with two accidents happening so close together, and my mum always told me these things came in threes. The staff were still on the boat and had clearly been busy. The chrome shone in the morning light and, apart from the mast, it was hard to tell what the boat had just been through.

I headed back to the hotel via the seawall, watching the wind and waves batter the coast below. As I walked into the dining room, I was surprised to see almost everyone except Jason and Alice were already down and tucking into breakfast. I joined them and poured myself a large cup of steaming coffee. Everyone was looking well rested this morning after a night in a bed that didn't keep moving.

'Daddy, what's the plan today?' asked Daisy.

'We have at least one day here while we wait for repairs, so we have a free day. We won't be leaving until tomorrow,' said Mike.

Daisy tugged on my arm. 'Let's go to Marrakech. I've always wanted to visit the medina and see the square in the old city.'

Nicholas overheard. Looking at me, he said, 'I'll go as well, Daisy.'

Disaster: there was no way I could avoid Nicholas joining us, but he was the last person I wanted to spend the day with. I thought Beth and Jane might come too, but Beth appeared to be under a dark cloud this morning that she blamed on a headache. I assumed it was something to do with the tears I'd seen the previous night. Jane said she would stay with Charlie in Essaouira. Mike said he'd rather lose his right nut than spend an hour in the medina, choking on fumes while being harassed by street sellers. He declared he'd spend the day looking after Beth. Jason would have to stay behind and rest up, but if I could get Alice to go it would break up the threesome of Nicholas, Daisy and me.

As we'd left the trip a bit late to organise, Nicholas suggested we spend the night in Marrakech and return the following morning. Daisy agreed, and I was left with little choice but to go along with them. After breakfast, Nicholas went off to organise a driver, get some local currency and find somewhere to stay while I searched for Alice.

Their room was at the end of the corridor, a few doors down from mine. I knocked gently in case they were sleeping. From beyond the door I heard Alice call out to come in.

The room was larger than mine. It had a separate sitting room with walls covered with a chic, washed-out turquoise finish that gave the impression of great age. The furniture was local, each piece either carved in wood or hand painted with intricate patterns and designs. The bedroom door was ajar and I could see Jason in bed sleeping. This room had the added benefit of a balcony where Alice was sitting. She looked completely relaxed as she enjoyed her tea in the morning sunshine.

She waved me over excitedly. 'Come and see this view, Summer.'

She stood up as I stepped out on to the balcony so I could reach her for a hug. Releasing her, I turned and took in the view. Perched above the main square, we could see across the town and down towards the harbour. Although you couldn't see the ocean from here due to the high sea walls, the sound of the waves crashing onto the rocks was clear above the morning bustle below. I closed my eyes and breathed in the warm salty air that gently caressed my face, trying to lock the image into my head.

I scraped an iron chair across the floor and sat down. Alice poured me a cup of mint tea from the intricate silver tea pot on its matching tray.

'Isn't this view amazing, Summer? I could sit here all day. You see down there? I've been watching that man with the white beard for a while now – I'm guessing he's sitting with his wife. He looks innocent enough at first glance, but you see where he is sitting, just by the passageway between those two buildings? The breeze whips through there – it's like a wind tunnel. As tourists walk past in their summer dresses, it hitches up their dresses. Then he looks over his wife's shoulder with his eyes bulging.' She offered me sugar.

I declined the sugar and joined Alice in watching this man. His eyes constantly moved left and right as he observed the women as they milled around the square. Somehow watching him watching them made me feel rather dirty. I looked away towards three local children running around a tree playing tag. 'How's Jason?' I asked as I sipped the tea.

'He didn't sleep too well, but I think he's asleep now. The doctor gave him a bottle of sleeping tablets just in case, and he took one this morning. The shock of the last few days has been a real strain on him. I'm worried about him – not just his physical self, but his mental state, I mean.'

'Alice, that's awful. I thought he looked reasonably upbeat when I saw him last night at the meal.'

'He did, didn't he? But when I came up to the room, he was already here and he looked shattered. He was laying on the bed in his clothes, staring at the ceiling fan,' she said, as she picked a piece of mint caught between her teeth. 'This trip hasn't really gone as we hoped, has it?'

'No,' I sighed. 'It hasn't quite turned out as expected. Poor Jason, he's had it worse than all of us and that's worried you sick. Hopefully a day onshore in a proper bed will help him get his head in better shape. Speaking of which, I'm going to go to Marrakech with Daisy and Nicholas this morning and staying there overnight. I was going to ask you to join us, but with Jason like this…?'

Alice perked up instantly. 'No, I could come. Jason will be

114

out of it for most of the day. The sleeping tablets are heavy duty, so he'll probably sleep for twenty-four hours. I might not get another chance to see Marrakech with you, so perhaps I should go.'

'Well, only if you feel up to it. But what about Jason?'

'I can write a note for him and ask the others to look in. It will be fine.' She jumped up. 'I'd better get changed and sort myself out. How long have I got?'

'We're leaving as soon as Nicholas has organised a driver. We just need a few overnight things. I'll ask the others to keep an eye on Jason while you get yourself sorted, and we'll meet in the lobby in an hour.'

'Okay, sweetie. See you soon.'

I went back to the breakfast room in search of the others. They were taking their time over breakfast; they probably had little planned beyond going for a walk while looking for somewhere interesting for lunch.

'Summer, you're back! I thought you were off to Marrakech.' Mike wiped pastry crumbs from his lips as the four of them looked at me.

'We are in a minute. Alice is coming with us, so we were wondering if you could check in on Jason throughout the day. He's taken a sleeping pill and Alice says he'll be fine after a good sleep, but I'd be more comfortable if I knew someone was keeping an eye on him.'

Beth turned away from me and looked out of the window, saying nothing. For a second no one spoke. The silence was broken by both Mike and Jane saying that of course they'd check on Jason. Jane even offered to sit with him while she read her book. 'Tell Alice not to worry, we'll keep watch over him between us. I need some shade today, so it's absolutely fine,' she said, smiling kindly at me.

Charlie backed up his wife, reassuring me that it wasn't a problem. Only Beth remained silent, and her sunglasses prevented me from reading her eyes.

We drove for two hours through a dry, fairly empty landscape with only the occasional small settlement. The roads were fast. I was taken aback by the endless lines of donkeys trekking along the dual carriageway, pulling carts still as if the twentieth century had never happened.

We stopped once on our journey to see the goats that were standing in the branches of some trees. It was a tourist trap, but one that Daisy was keen to see. It was said that the goats used to climb into the lower branches of the trees to forage for the berries. That may have been true once, but these goats hadn't climbed up there themselves; they had clearly been placed there by the farmer who demanded money from anyone who stopped to be photographed with the poor animals.

We stood there for several minutes. Under the blazing sun all day next to a busy road, these animals were being exploited. Being no better than the dozens of other tourists around us, we took photos and paid the farmer a few dirham before continuing our journey.

As we approached Marrakesh, the streets began to fill with people and cars, there were more buildings and the noise level rose. The taxi driver was taking us straight to a riad just inside the ancient walls of the medina. He pulled up in a small dusty car park, where we all disembarked and grabbed our small overnight bags. Only Alice struggled with a case that was more suited to a family holiday.

I wasn't sure why Nicholas had joined us because he'd shown little interest in any of us for the past week. Was he here to look out for his little sister? It didn't seem likely; there seemed to be little sibling love between them. Boredom and the draw of a day in Marrakesh must have forced him to join us.

As we picked up our bags and looked around us, a tall, slim man appeared. 'Riad Orchard Fragrance. Please follow me and allow me to take your case.' He smiled and took the case from Alice. 'I am Karim and I will take you to the riad.'

We followed him as he strode off towards a narrow passageway. It wasn't wide enough for cars but evidently suitable for mopeds and bikes to squeeze by us at speed. The path narrowed further; at points we had to duck down to pass under the beams that hung under rooms built over the path. They created small tunnels that were a real problem for Alice, who had to bend down continually.

Just as I could see Daisy getting a little nervous about where we were being taken, we stopped outside a large, richly carved wooden door. A smaller door in the centre of it opened and we followed our guide inside.

From outside the riad looked like a dusty old building but inside was a revelation. There was a small lobby, then we entered a central area that reached up three storeys high. In the middle was a pool lit with a soft turquoise light, not for swimming but seemingly a focal point. Water gently rolled over stones into the pool, giving the whole area a feeling of calm after the hectic streets outside. Tables were arranged in twos and fours around the pool for guests to eat at. Above us, the bedrooms were arranged around this atrium. The western influence of our previous hotel had gone, and I now felt as if we were in a more authentic Moroccan setting.

There was no standing around at a reception desk to check in here. Kariam sat us down and served mint tea and pastries while he gave us an introduction to the hotel and maps and guides to Marrakech. He pointed out places of interest and how to avoid getting lost in the maze of the medina, with its labyrinth of narrow pathways, vibrant souks and picture-perfect courtyards. Then he gave us each a padlock and took us to our rooms.

There were four rooms on each floor, each facing into the atrium. We were on the second floor, looking down onto the tranquil pool. Each room was behind shuttered doors and I could now see what the padlocks were for, to lock each room from the outside when leaving.

Daisy was very excited; this place was different to anywhere she'd stayed before. After I'd checked that she was happy to sleep in a room on her own, I opened my doors and looked inside. There was one large room with a bathroom hidden behind more shuttered doors. It was simply furnished with a small coffee table and an Oriental sofa covered with burgundy-coloured cushions. The walls had that same paint-washed effect as the hotel in Essaouira, but here the cracks and flaking paint looked genuine. A few years earlier a room like this would have been considered shabby; now it had the shabby-chic look that everyone paid extra for. The bed was half hidden under a mountain of beautifully patterned pillows, with one large, deep cushion that acted as a headboard.

As I was going to check out the bathroom, Daisy appeared at the door. 'Summer, can we go out now? If there really are thousands of stalls, we'd best get started.'

'Yes, get the others and we can head off. Meet you downstairs in five minutes.'

We waited beside the pool for a quarter of an hour before Alice came down. She'd changed from jeans into a summer dress that didn't make it half way down to her knees, or cover much at the top either.

Nicholas was the first to comment. 'You do know this is a Muslim country and it's respectful to dress conservatively?'

'This is Marrakech. I'm sure they've seen women in a dress before,' Alice retorted. 'It will be fine. Let's go.'

I was wearing a long cotton dress, while Daisy wore a pair of light-green spotted trousers. As the four of us set off, men kept glancing – or at times glaring – our way. It was Alice who was drawing their attention and seemingly enjoying pushing the boundaries as we made our way through the narrow streets.

The medina is a market like no other, one of the world's greatest mazes. Maps were useless; the labyrinth of passage-ways continually branched off in random directions, almost deliberately designed to confuse and disorientate. As we wandered between the stalls, constantly dodging speeding motorbikes and small mopeds that wove through the crowds, we couldn't help being impressed at the riders' skill in avoiding collisions.

We allowed ourselves to get lost amongst the stalls. Daisy took the lead, buying obscure items that appeared to be chosen based on their colour. Alice enjoyed the browsing and haggling as much as Daisy, leaving me with Nicholas.

I'd expected him to wander off on his own rather than drag around with his sister and the two of us, but he seemed content to hang back. He picked up the odd item, asking for a price in French, which all the traders seemed to speak, and then raising his eyebrows before putting it back down.

I resisted talking to him, wary that he might bite my head off. It felt strange to spend an afternoon with him and not talk. He had no reason to dislike me that I could think of, yet he made no effort to be polite. I often caught him looking at me and then quickly looking away without saying anything, which made me even more uncomfortable. He really was a strange guy. Ever since he'd corrected me about how he wanted me to pronounce his name, I'd been cautious around him.

After several hours of wandering, dusk was creeping in. The narrow, covered walkways became more magical as the sunlight gave way to the traders' lamps and lights. After passing through yet another passage lined with vendors selling items identical to all the rest, I was starting to think that finding our way out was going to prove a problem. Then we found ourselves in a narrow street that gradually widened and led us into Jemaa el-Fna square, famed for its snake charmers and local folk dancers.

'By luck more than judgement, we seem to have found our way to Jemma el-Fna,' Nicholas said. 'I don't know about you, girls, but I'm starving and really fancy trying a tagine. Shall we find a restaurant with a good rooftop view so we can watch the square while we eat?'

We all nodded and followed him around the edge of the square, looking at the remarkably similar restaurants that all offered us tagine-based meals. We settled on one that had a roof garden with a view over the most interesting part of the square. It was crammed with men carrying monkeys on their shoulders, looking for tourists who wanted to have their photograph taken for a fee. Small groups of musicians were playing separately but close together, creating a wall of sound that drifted across the square.

After a short wait, we managed to get a table on the outer edge of the balcony. The waiter saw we were looking cold; Alice, in particular, was now shivering in her summer dress as the heat of the day quickly evaporated, leaving the air chill. Calling on a fellow waiter, he moved a space heater from another table, much to the displeasure of the couple sitting there, and delivered it to our table. I'd always had a problem with space heaters – it seemed to be a waste to heat up the night sky – but that night I put my green leanings to one side and accepted the warmth with gratitude.

The menus were passed around. After a few minutes of quiet contemplation, Alice said, 'So, what type of tagine do we all want? Not much choice if you aren't a fan of food cooked in pots. I'm tempted by the salad, but I'm not sure about salads when I'm outside Europe. You never know what the water is like that they wash it in.'

'Let's just order four different tagines and share.' Nicholas closed his menu, having decided already that we would go along with him. Alice agreed and Daisy followed her lead, so Nicholas ordered while I said nothing.

I was already uncomfortable with Nicholas. I kept catching him studying me, but if I went to catch his eye he looked away. I thought about striking up a conversation with him beyond comments such as 'can you pass the salt, please', but held back. He'd been the rude one, he'd blanked me and left me squirming, so I wasn't going to risk humiliation again by trying to break the silence.

While we waited for our food, we watched the entertainment below. Large groups of tourists and locals encircled the most popular entertainers, while the snake charmers and monkey photographers plied their trade and looked for individuals who were ready to exchange money for an exotic photo to share on Facebook.

As Daisy was taking photos of all the madness, I suddenly

realised I'd scarcely taken a single photo during the trip. I looked around for the waiter, called him over and asked him if he would take a picture of the four of us. We were leaning in together so we could get the square in the background when I felt an arm on my shoulder. I turned; Nicholas had draped his arm casually around me just as the photo was being taken.

We shifted back into our seats and thanked the waiter. I took my phone and checked the image. The photo was spoiled because he'd caught me as I turned my head to look at the hand that had suddenly appeared. I looked at Nicholas's expression. As he'd pulled me in close, he'd had a smile on his face that I hadn't seen before, a genuine, joyous smile.

Chapter 27

After

I t was getting late, and I was about to turn in. The holiday experience had been lost for us since Jason's death; rather than sitting around chatting, playing cards and drinking ridiculous amounts, we'd retreated into our own little bubbles. We talked quietly one to one but without the laughter that had filled the boat at the start of the journey.

I picked up my glass of water and went on deck to collect my book from my sun lounger. As I slid open the deck door, I was surprised to see Beth sitting with her arms folded on the balustrade. Her head was resting on her arms and she was looking out into the distance.

She hadn't heard me, and I thought about stepping back inside and leaving her in peace, but I wanted to talk to her and knew that this might be my only chance. I crossed the deck, sat a short distance away and waited. When she didn't look up or acknowledge me, I said, 'It's a beautiful evening, isn't it?'

It was perfect, with a clear sky and a full moon creating an enormous pool of white light on the rippling water. Beth turned to look at me and said, 'Is it?'

She wasn't clearly visible in the moonlight but, from what

I could see, she looked terrible. Her eyes were bloodshot and she wore no makeup; she looked ten years older than when we'd set sail. She turned her head and continued to stare at the horizon.

'We've missed you these last few days,' I said. 'I was getting worried about you.'

Beth didn't show any sign of hearing me.

'It's been a terrible time for us all. I've not known Jason long, but it hit me hard. I know what it's like to lose someone you love out of the blue. The shock feels like a punch in the stomach. Accepting that someone can be here one minute and gone the next is so hard. It does get easier though – the cliché is true that time heals. Knowing someone took their own life is harder still. It leaves you angry, as well heartbroken.'

Beth turned to look at me. 'He didn't. Jason wouldn't have taken his own life. No way.'

'What makes you so sure of that?' I asked.

'Because I've known Jason, known him for a long time. He had problems, but he never saw anything as hopeless. Only someone without hope would commit suicide.'

'I understand that you've been friends with Jason for a while now. How did you guys meet?'

Beth sucked on her top lip. 'You want the story, don't you? The investigative reporter, never off duty,' she said, not unkindly. 'I heard you've been asking a lot of questions. Well, you're in luck this time because I want to speak. Mike told me you were asking questions, that you were suspicious that Jason didn't kill himself. That makes two of us because I know Jason. I *knew* Jason,' she corrected herself. 'He wouldn't let problems bring him down. Everything life threw at him was a problem to be solved. Things were tough for him over the money, but he'd already found a way forward. He told me that when we were in Morocco.'

'You're right, I am suspicious about his death. It seems out of character the more I learn about him. Alice doesn't believe it was suicide, either.'

'Doesn't she?' Beth raised her eyebrows.

The lounge area light was switched off inside; now we were illuminated only by the safety lights and the moon.

'Tell me, how did you and Jason meet?' I asked again.

'It was a weird chance meeting, the sort that sometimes happens in life. I'd just arrived in Antibes for a charity fundraiser. I was sitting alone in a cafe near the harbour, reading a book. Jason was seated a table away from me. I noticed him because he kept gazing my way. I'm very attuned to men's attention – I often travel alone and receiving unwanted attention is one of the drawbacks.

'Jason was handsome and certainly younger than average, so I was surprised when he came across and asked me about my book. He'd read it too and so, after talking about it for a while, I asked him to join me. I'd normally have brushed off an advance like that, but I was enjoying the novel and happy to chat about it for a few minutes. We chatted for more than an hour. I found him articulate and easy to talk to, and he made me laugh.

'The whole time he was with me, all the conversation was above board. There was no seduction going on. This was no pickup; he was only looking for company. After an hour or so, he took a phone call from work and said he had to leave. As he stood up, I asked him to dine with me that evening. It was a spur of the moment thing. He hesitated and told me he was married, but he'd enjoyed the conversation so saw no harm in talking more.'

I wasn't sure how much of this story to believe. It sounded plausible – Jason was friendly, and I could imagine him killing time by talking to someone. But somehow it sounded a bit too innocent – a chance meeting, two married people talking books in a romantic cafe on the Cote d'Azur. But as Beth seemed up for talking, I didn't interrupt.

'We met at one of those restaurants where the view of the harbour made up for the poor service and average food. We enjoyed a bottle of Bastide Blanche Rosé, ate canapés and red mullet, and talked about culture and art. All the things Mike has no interest in. I knew Jason was married, but it wasn't important. We shared a connection that evening, and we became friends over that weekend.'

It was definitely an edited version of the story and I didn't believe a word of it. I wondered if this was the story Beth had told Mike.

'If you were away on your own, when did Mike and Jason meet?'

'Jason and I stayed in touch and met occasionally for lunch if we were both free. One lunchtime he was extremely excited and bought an expensive bottle of champagne. It seemed he was celebrating a series of investments that had just paid off handsomely and he'd received a substantial bonus. His excitement rubbed off on me. As he explained in more detail what he did, I realised that maybe he could do the same for us one day.

'I'm not greedy though,' she added. 'It wasn't like that. Mike always complained that he was paying a fortune for investment advice that appeared to give him returns that only covered the fees. Jason seemed like the perfect answer. I knew he loved the same football team as Mike and seemed to like cricket as well. Men are such one-dimensional beings – it was obvious that they'd hit it off.

'I couldn't tell Mike how I'd met Jason because he might not have understood how innocent it all was, so I arranged for Jason to come to Geneva for a motor show where I could introduce them. I made sure the topics of football and cricket came up. Without prompting, Mike invited Jason to a match with him.'

Beth's eyes were welling up and she stopped talking to wipe a tear from her cheek. 'That was the start of a friendship and later a business relationship that was very successful until recently.'

'Why are you telling me this if you kept it from your husband? Why would you trust me not to say anything?' I asked, puzzled by her apparent honesty.

'Alice knows about how Jason and I met – he told me when we were in Morocco. He said it in a way that makes me think she always knew. It was only a friendship, but I find it strange that she never let on to me that she knew. I would have expected some coldness or a warning to keep my hands off, but it never happened. Either she never saw me as a threat to their relationship, or she was happy for Jason to be my friend because it suited her at the time. I'm not likely to ask her, not now, but I'd love to know what went on.'

I still wasn't sure which bits of her story to believe. The whole situation was strange, and her relationship with Alice while all this was going on was remarkable.

Beth stuck to the line that it was platonic, and possibly it was. She may well have fallen heavily for Jason and simply lived in hope that one day he would leave Alice. All the while he was stringing her along, using her to stay close to Mike. Alice never struck me as the type to tolerate an open marriage, so possibly Jane and Charlie were wrong and it was more innocent than it seemed.

'I saw you crying in Essaouira after you'd been talking to Jason. Was that when he told you that Alice knew, and things had to be broken off?'

Beth went quiet and I thought she was going to clam up, but she composed herself. 'Jason told me that Alice knew about our friendship. She'd given him no choice but to end it. He told me that he had a plan to make everything right for us all. If I seemed upset, it was because we'd been friends for a long time and I relied on my relationship with Jason to retain my sanity.

'Mike and I have two things in common, Nicholas and Daisy. Mike adores me, I know that, but he couldn't tell you why. We have nothing to talk about beyond the children. That's no life for either of us, but Mike would have killed Jason if he'd known…'

She tailed off as she realised what she was saying and sighed. 'Look, I lost Jason twice in the space of a couple of days. I thought that us not being friends any longer was a pain I couldn't bear, and then he died. Jason struggled to speak to me, kept crying when he said it. He was in a fragile state, I know that, but he wasn't suicidal. He had no reason to break up with me if he planned to kill himself a couple of days later.'

'True, but suicide isn't always planned. It can be a spur of the moment reaction to a seemingly desperate situation,' I countered.

'Of course, but Jason was positive and upbeat. He was bristling with ideas about how he was going to get out of this financial disaster. He didn't share them with me, but he had them alright and his eyes were shining. I'll never know what his plans were, but I'd like to think they involved me.'

Chapter 28

Before

The food came, four sizzling, steaming, terracotta pots filled with bubbling meats and soft stewed vegetables. Daisy talked to me, picking out things that were going on in the square in her excitable young voice. Some teenagers are shy around adults and sit sullenly, too scared or uninterested to speak to a grown up, but Daisy had no such qualms. She spoke to me as if I were her best friend – and she did like to talk.

Nicholas was talking to Alice. He struggled to say hello to me but happily chatted away to her. Between Daisy's constant chatter, the sounds rising up from the square and the call to prayer from the mosque, I wasn't paying them too much attention, but I heard Nicholas speak about an argument he'd overheard.

'I heard Jason in a very fruity discussion with Yasmin. I was there on the deck on a sun lounger, headphones on, with my back to them. They either didn't notice me or thought I was listening to something, but I could hear much of what they were saying. Yasmin said, "Don't take it out on me." Jason said something about maintenance bills for the boat that didn't add up and how, if he mentioned them to Mike, her gravy train would be over. She shoved him up against the side of the cabin and told him to keep his dick out of mouths where they didn't belong. Jason went quiet. I don't think he was expecting that.'

I looked at Alice's face, unsure what to make of it. I couldn't imagine Yasmin saying those words, but then I didn't know her that well.

She said, 'Is that so? He did mention something to me about a run-in with Yasmin and called her a "fleecing bitch", but that was during the meal before the storm. I didn't think much about it.'

'Well I thought about it, after Jason got lumped on the back of the head,' Nicholas retorted. 'I was going to talk to my father about it, see if he knew what Jason was talking about, but we've not been on the best of terms. I'm sure Yasmin is inflating the invoices, helping herself to a bit extra. Everyone does that with my father.'

I couldn't imagine Jason ever using the word 'bitch' for anyone because he was far too well mannered, but maybe in private with Alice he was different. I guessed he never told Mike about the money, because Mike would have brought it up when he was fuming about the storm and blaming Yasmin.

I really wanted to ask whether this argument had happened before or after the diving accident, but I decided not to let on that I'd heard the conversation in case I fired up Nicholas's temper.

'So are you going to speak to your dad about Yasmin?' said Alice, playing with the straw in her Coke.

'Right now, probably not. We're not getting on, in many ways thanks to Jason. Repeating it to my father will make it look like I'm trying to cause trouble for Jason via Yasmin. Jason has caused me lots of problems lately, and I don't want my father thinking I have some sort of vendetta against him. I've no idea what he was talking about, so he can raise it with my father. He'll be looking for ways to get back into Dad's good books.'

'When exactly was this row?' Alice asked.

'The day before the scuba dive.'

Chapter 29

After

The wind was up, and a gentle patter of rain swept across the cabin window. The skies had grown heavy with clouds for the last hour and my cabin was dark. I switched on the desk lamp and turned the page of my notebook. I'd started to make notes of my conversations, trying to piece together the events of the last few days to build some understanding of Jason and what may have led to his death.

Suicide was looking more improbable, but the alternative was far scarier. If I believed that it *wasn't* suicide then I was in the middle of the ocean with a killer, a ruthless killer who went to great lengths to make a murder look like a suicide.

When I'd first met Jason as we set off in London for Monte Carlo, I thought he was the perfect husband – charming, attractive, smart and kind, much loved. Yet somehow he seemed to have upset everyone. Mike lost a fortune thanks to him and he could have known that something was going on between Jason and Beth. Nicholas lost his father's investment in his business venture and blamed Jason. Beth appeared to have been having an affair with him, whether it was physical or not, which had made Jane angry on Mike's behalf. Even

Yasmin, who hardly knew Jason, had had a run in with him.

While everyone might have some sort of motive, the means to kill Jason bothered me. Somehow he had ended up in the water with a noose around his neck, strangled as he was dragged along behind us. If he was murdered, how did the killer get the rope around his neck? Jason wasn't the biggest guy but, even so, how could someone have got him over the side without a struggle? I hadn't noticed any other injuries beyond the massive trauma to the neck, but then I hadn't been looking for any.

Jason was being stored in the freezer below, carefully wrapped in a body bag. There was an option to bury him at sea, but when Yasmin called the authorities they told her to bring his body in to land. He should only be buried at sea as a last resort if there was nowhere to store him safely.

Alice had wanted a burial at sea and had argued with Yasmin, fighting back her tears as she tried to convince her and Mike that it was what Jason would have wanted. She said she couldn't bear to be at sea knowing that Jason's body was below deck. But Yasmin had stood her ground and Mike had backed her up. As captain, Yasmin couldn't disobey a clear instruction and perform a burial at sea, especially as there was no need to. Jason's body could be returned home for a proper funeral.

The rain was easing now and sunlight returned through the porthole, flooding the cabin with light again. I needed to take a closer look at Jason's body, so I went up on deck to find Yasmin. She was at the helm in her brilliant yellow waterproofs, silhouetted against a stunning double rainbow. The lower part of it had faded, the colours washed out, but the top half was a wash of vivid colours, dazzling in their brightness.

I pointed them out to Yasmin, and she turned and stood with

me in wonder for a few moments. Then I said, 'Yasmin, I need to take a look at Jason's body.'

She looked at me inquisitively. 'Why on earth would you want to see Jason? I can't just let you in like that.'

'I need to check something. It won't take a moment. I know this is unusual, but it is important.'

'It certainly is unusual, and I can't let you. Jason died at sea. Until a doctor has seen him and produced a death certificate, his body has to remain undisturbed.'

'I wouldn't ask if it wasn't important. I'll only be a couple of minutes and you're welcome to be there as well, just to confirm I'm not up to anything.'

'Sorry, it's just not possible. I was instructed to keep the body secured until we reach the authorities.'

I couldn't make out her eyes behind her dark glasses, but I was sure she was holding my gaze, not budging from her position. 'Maybe you could help me with something else,' I said slowly. 'Somebody overheard an argument between you and Jason. Do you want to tell me about that?'

Yasmin stood still, pondering a response. Finally she said, 'I spoke with Jason a number of times. An argument, though? No, we never argued. We had no reason to.'

'Really? You don't recall a row over inflated invoices that got quite heated and ended physically?'

'Physically? No! Jason had got the wrong end of the stick on a couple of matters, things that were frankly none of his business, and I told him so. But it was nothing and blew over.' Her North African accent became stronger as her voice became more strained.

'Blew over in that Jason conveniently died? Look, I'm not interested in invoices, and I see no reason to raise the subject, but I do need to see Jason's body.'

'The invoices were inflated, but not by me. It was a member of the crew, and it's a matter I've dealt with. I saw no reason to involve Mike because the amount was not significant.'

'I'm not here to blackmail you,' I said. 'I think you want the truth to come out as much as I do.'

'Seeing Jason's body is a waste of time. There is nothing other than the horrible injuries around his neck. But, if you insist, I suppose looking will do no harm if I'm with you.'

Yasmin fiddled around putting the yacht onto autopilot and we set off below decks. On the way we passed Daisy, who asked what I was up to. It made me jumpy, as if I were doing something wrong, even though it was only a casual question. I brushed her off by saying that I'd see her up on the sun loungers.

The freezer where Jason was stored had been padlocked shut. It was a small, walk-in freezer, like a pantry, but deep enough to hold Jason's body. As Yasmin unlocked and opened the door, the frozen air immediately began to escape.

The sight of the body bag jolted me, and I had to steady myself before walking in. I knelt down beside it and pulled the zip down its entire length, revealing Jason. He was still dressed for dinner, his formal shirt ripped open presumably by the pressure of the water tearing off a button as he was dragged behind the yacht. His dark trousers were still okay, but he was wearing only one deck shoe. I assumed he'd lost the other in the water. Strangely, the deck shoes were slip-ons; they didn't go with his more formal dinner clothes.

Chapter 30

Before

As the sun provided a stunning sunset over the minaret, the atmosphere in the square changed. More tourists flooded in to find food; mingling amongst the entertainers, they sought out something that appeared a little dangerous or new. From our table above the square, the aroma from the dozens of restaurants around us was pungent with a mix of spices.

We finished our meal and spent the next hour exploring. We stuck together as we wandered around, stopping here and there to listen to the traditional music. Daisy was a street-vendor's dream, happy to pay for a snake charmer or have a monkey climb all over her as she had her photo taken ready to be instantly uploaded onto Instagram.

Nicholas continued to chat intermittently with Alice, and even joked with Daisy a couple of times, while avoiding any conversation with me. I caught him looking at my legs more than once. His silence was beginning to rankle, but I held back from saying anything. I was beginning to wonder if he had a problem talking to all women or had just taken an instant dislike to me.

After a while Alice declared she was getting tired and wanted to head back to the riad; the others agreed, albeit reluctantly, that if one went we should all go. As we walked back through the packed market, Alice took my hand and pulled me over to a stall stacked impossibly high with fresh dates. She asked the vendor in French if she could try a couple of different types, then turned to me. 'So how is it going with Nicholas? I've not seen you talk to him, but he can't keep his eyes off of you.'

I feigned surprise, although I'd wondered if his sly glances were part of some crush. Private-school boys seemed to behave in one of two ways with girls, either arrogant and overbearing, expecting every girl to fall to their knees before them, or painfully shy with no idea how to talk to somebody they liked. I guessed my age would only add to Nicholas's lack of confidence. I was certainly not interested in him, so I had no intention of helping him out by breaking the ice. 'I really think you've misread this one,' I said. 'He's been nothing but rude and a complete arse towards me this trip. If he did like me for some reason, he has a damned childish way of showing it.'

'He is fucking loaded, though. Think about the holidays you'd get. Imagine the birthday presents.'

I hoped Alice was joking, but I couldn't always be sure with her. I knew her world revolved around money, but she knew that mine didn't. I would never have dreamt of dating someone for their money.

'Seriously, when did you last date?' she persisted. 'You're too young to be a widow forever. I know how hard it's been for you, but you need to move on. Nicholas is here – it wouldn't hurt you to dip your toe in. Don't be like you were on our last holiday!'

Our last holiday together had been a fortnight on a Greek

island. We'd gone together, but Alice had ditched me again and again. Whenever anyone was willing to buy the drinks, she was game. I was happy to spend time alone, but I still felt abandoned by her.

I remembered her snide comments about me not getting the same level of attention that she was. She couldn't see that I wasn't giving off the 'available' vibe to any drunk at the bar.

That holiday was the moment I realised that Alice and I would stay in touch but she was no longer central to my life. I would never be able to rely on her as you could on a true friend. She had called when I lost Tom, full of kind words and promises to be by my side. The reality was that she was there when the TV news crews arrived, always ready to speak for me on camera. She portrayed herself as the loyal, devoted friend, but when the cameras vanished and the news story moved on so did Alice.

'I'm not closed to meeting someone else. I miss Tom every day, but I know he's not coming back and I can let him go. I'll meet someone else, but it certainly won't be for their money – and it won't be a rich ex-public-school boy who can't communicate with females!'

'It's your life. Just don't forget to live it.'

'Thanks for your concern,' I said sarcastically, as I popped a mouth-watering soft date into my mouth.

Daisy came up behind us and helped herself to one. 'Wow, these are lush. I'm going to buy a box for Daddy. Alice, could you buy me two boxes? I'm out of money and I doubt they'll take a card.'

Alice pulled out her sparkly purse from her DK shoulder bag and paid with a two-hundred dinah note, before waiting for the five dinah change. She put the boxes of dates in her bag, while Daisy ran across to get Nicholas. We set off back towards the riad, dodging the motor bikes, feeling exhausted now from hours of shopping and wandering the streets and lanes. Nicholas stayed a few steps behind me, never attempting to speak to me.

In the morning I awoke early, even though my riad room had no outside window and my room was in an inky darkness. As I opened the door and looked down, the dining area was dark, illuminated only by the pool lights. I realised that there was no natural light anywhere in the riad, not a single window. Were they all like this?

I could hear the staff moving around already, busy preparing breakfast at the back. I threw on some warm clothes, grabbed a book and headed upstairs where I'd been told there was a roof garden.

The roof was less of a garden and more of a terrace, with potted plants and an olive tree growing in an enormous terracotta pot. As I stepped out, the call to prayer started up, lyrical and mournful, falling over the city and calling believers to the mosque.

The sun was rising and I could see across much of the city. Coloured by an orange haze, it was a sea of TV aerials and washing lines, with minarets rising above the clutter. In the distance, Marrakesh was almost completely encircled by mountains. I wondered why this spot, which didn't have a river running through it, had been chosen to build a city. Our time here had been too brief, and I'd seen and learnt too little about the place. I would have to return one day and do it justice.

Chapter 31

Having finished my book, I let my eyes close and tried to doze. What I should have been doing was some sort of workout to get rid of the extra weight I seemed to be carrying. I hadn't started the holiday with a bikini body and had made matters worse by sitting around all day and snacking out of boredom. The food we'd been served was first-class, but rich in calories as well as flavour – and I didn't even want to think about how many calories I'd drunk.

After Tom died I'd lost weight for months, but part of my recovery process was regaining my appetite. I'd always preferred to feel healthy; looking fit was something I hadn't thought about too much. But just after I'd been offered my first TV show, I realised I was in no shape to keep up with the demands of the schedule. I set about a fitness routine, taking up running and going to spinning classes twice a week. By the time filming started, I had clawed back some of my vigour and had tried to keep it up ever since.

Now I felt bloated. I couldn't switch off, so I decided to try a small workout. I looked around and checked I was alone, then sluggishly rolled off the lounger and lay on the deck. The wood was hot, scorched by the sun even with the constant breeze, and I lay for a few moments waiting for my back to get used to the temperature before doing some sit-ups.

I'd always been jealous of those who love exercise and get a buzz from it; for me it was a means to an end. I'd finish a run with friends, battling mud, rain and hypothermia, and when we finally stopped, exhausted and cold, they would be, 'Wow, wasn't that amazing?' I always wanted to scream, 'No, it was horrible! My legs are burning and all I can think about is a hot bath.'

I put in my earbuds and tried to decide what other exercises I could do that would increase my heart rate. I set about doing star jumps and running on the spot, trying to go faster and faster, setting my pace to the music, keeping it going right to the end of the song.

Finally I slumped down onto the lounger. As I caught my breath, sweat oozed out of my pores. I rubbed my face with the towel to try and stop it stinging my eyes.

'I have some weights in my room if you want to use them.'

I jumped and dropped the towel at the sound of the voice. Nicholas was standing on the balcony above me, picking pomegranate seeds out one at a time with a toothpick.

'And I wasn't watching you, by the way,' he said.

He made his way down while I slipped a dress over my damp bikini. Standing in the shade next to me, he blurted out a compliment about the dress. It was a pretty white slip, nothing special and certainly not designer wear, and I felt that he was trying to think of an icebreaker. When I smiled and thanked him, he let out the breath he'd been holding and relaxed a little.

The way he spoke to me was a little disconcerting: shy, with fleeting glances. 'I keep meaning to say, I feel like I was rude to you and we got off to a bad start.' His voice was halting, nervous.

'Yes, I agree,' I said. 'It wasn't the best introduction I've had. In my line of work, I get to meet many people who take an instant dislike to me, but I hadn't expected it on this trip.'

'I should have said something before. I can only apologize if I made you feel uncomfortable. It wasn't my intention, but this hasn't been an easy trip for me. I'm not trying to make excuses, but—'

'Sounds like you are to me,' I cut in.

Nicholas flinched at my response, clearly not used to women standing up to him. He hadn't been pleasant towards me, and I didn't want to hear excuses or lame apologies. At the same time, I did need to talk to him in case he'd anything worth telling me about Jason.

I softened my voice and smiled. 'We all have bad days.'

He seemed to relax, the tension falling from his shoulders as he picked up a butter knife and started scraping at the pomegranate, trying to loosen some more seeds. 'I wanted to apologise when we were in Marrakech, but I never seemed to find the right opportunity or get you on your own. I should have done it before we went scuba diving but I felt awful, like everyone was blaming me for what happened.'

'Jason nearly died and you were the only person with him, so obviously you're going to feel bad. Do you feel guilty about it?'

'I should have looked back and checked on him, noticed that he wasn't there. Well yes, I feel guilty about that.'

'You weren't looking for a little payback?'

'You mean did I know about the lost money? No, absolutely not. I found out about that after the dive.'

He offered me a drink, which I refused. What was it with

these people and their drinking? It seemed that it was never too early to start, although with Nicholas it looked more like he needed Dutch courage.

He stepped inside for a moment before returning with a beer, already wet from condensation. He indicated the seat next to me and I nodded.

'I knew there was something up with Jason. He looked like the blue-eyed boy, smart and charming with his beautiful wife, impressing my father and persuading him that his fortune was safe in his hands. Even before he lost all that money, I knew there was something not right. I didn't know exactly what he was up to, but I learnt enough in business school to know that nobody gets it right all the time. For every winner, there has to be a loser. Jason had been on a good run and I thought his confidence would be his undoing. You don't flip a coin and get it right every time, and that's what he was doing. When you bet on currency movements, data, charts and fundamentals can give you an edge if you read them right, but it's still fifty-fifty in the long run. Either they go up or they go down.'

'So Jason bet on black and the ball landed on red?'

'Yes, but that happens every day. His problem was he geared up, borrowed money to bet with, and he didn't hedge his bet. His cockiness nearly destroyed us. It meant that there was no protection in place if the bet went sour. He risked us losing it all. It seems like simple good fortune and luck prevented us from being wiped out, but there were big losses.'

'Sounds like reason enough to leave him out there to drown.'

'Plenty of reason, for sure – except I really didn't know about the losses then. When we went diving, I still thought he was just a bit of a git, worming his way into my father's life by charming my mother. Don't think I didn't see what was going on between those two. She might be my mother, but I saw the way she looked at him, how she laughed at his jokes.'

I waited, leaving a long silence in the hope he would say more. If he really saw something between his mum and Jason, that alone might be reason enough to abandon Jason at sea even if he wasn't trying to kill him.

Finally I said, 'Jason adored Alice and would do anything for her. He might have been friendly with Beth, but that would be all. Alice loved Jason but she's the jealous type. She'd have murdered him herself if she thought he had eyes for anyone else.'

He turned towards me and examined my face. 'Your friendship with Alice may be blinding you. My father might not have seen it, but Jane did. I used to watch her virtually steaming when she saw the two of them together. You know Jane loves my father, don't you? She always has. She told me once when I was little – she thought I wouldn't understand, wouldn't remember. She's like a lovesick puppy who's followed him around for years under the guise of working for him. I'm not sure my father notices that he's in this ridiculous love loop where everyone adores someone who's not their partner. It was like Prince Charles being married to Diana, but not knowing that Camilla was waiting in the wings – except I really don't think my father was aware of what was going on and I'm sure Charlie knew. Charlie didn't say anything, though, because he wanted to keep the peace. He enjoys the benefits of their friendship with Mike, so he keeps quiet.'

Nicholas had gone from silent to full rant within minutes. If he was right, the situation was a mess in so many ways. Mike would have had another reason to hate Jason if he'd suspected something was going on between him and Beth. But there was also Jane; how far would she go to avenge the man she clearly loved?

While nobody had talked about Jason's death being anything other than suicide, the number of people who had reason to do him harm kept growing. Was Nicholas's outburst a flare to distract attention away from himself and his own motives?

There was one other area I needed to explore, but it would take a more gentle tack. 'You seemed very angry with Jason when he blocked your dad's investment in your business start-up. I felt sorry for you. It seemed from where I was sitting that Jason shouldn't have had any input – it was between you and your dad.'

'Too right. It wasn't his bloody place, sticking his nose in where it wasn't required. It wouldn't have mattered, though. My father never likes my ideas, and he used Jason's reasoning as an excuse. Dad forgets that his father might have started with nothing, but mine didn't. All those millions came from his father's hard work. Dad might have been working from the age of ten or something stupid, but he never started from scratch. Why he thinks I should is beyond me.'

Chapter 32

Before

We left Marrakesh after breakfast and drove in silence through city streets that were already bustling. Nicholas sat away from me, looking out of his window while I stared out of my mine. In the reflection, I occasionally caught him turning to look at me for a brief moment.

As we travelled out of the city and the streets became less packed with people and traffic, my mind turned to Jason. I wondered if he was feeling better after a day's rest. When I'd asked after him over breakfast, Alice said she'd not heard from him.

It was strange, but I hadn't met Jason before this trip. I wasn't in close contact with Alice in the years after college. When the wedding invitation had arrived shortly after Tom's death, I wasn't in a good place and in no state of mind to attend such a joyful occasion. I'd put away my grief long enough to send a card wishing Alice every happiness, but then returned to my dark days. Over the next few years our contact was minimal, with half-hearted promises to meet up added to our annual Christmas card. Our lives had taken different paths and, although I knew we'd probably always stay in touch, there wasn't enough of a relationship there to make me want to pursue a closer friendship.

Jason, though, was not what I had anticipated. A reflection of Alice no doubt, but I had expected Jason to be someone I would struggle to like. Knowing Alice and her single-minded drive for status and money, I had quite naturally assumed that Jason, being a financial advisor, would be a bit of a sleaze bag. Most money men that I'd come into contact with seemed to share certain traits, from the shiny suit to over-familiarity. They were always on duty, constantly on the lookout for a new client.

Jason was atypical. He had an easy charm, he clearly adored Alice and I could see what had attracted her to him. It was strange, therefore, that she didn't know how Jason was doing and seemed unconcerned, not displaying any anxieties about the lack of news. Either she was confident that he would be fine, or she was good at hiding her feelings.

We arrived back in Essaouira just before midday and headed straight down to the boatyard. The others had already checked out of the hotel and were on the yacht. Jason was sitting on deck in the shade drinking iced water, but he stood up when we arrived to hug Alice. I watched her as they embraced and she kissed his forehead gently over and over again.

Beth and Mike joined us and there were stiff greetings for Nicholas. Only Daisy seemed to get any warmth from her dad as he hugged her. How strange these people were. Mike shook my hand and said he was pleased to have us all back together. The yacht was fixed, Jason was recovered, and we were ready to set off again. 'Yasmin, let's get us going. Antigua awaits! Lunch in one hour.'

The four of us headed below to our cabins. As I opened my door, I felt Nicholas's eyes on me from down the corridor but I didn't look back.

The meal was relaxed and jovial as Daisy entertained us with the story of our visit to Marrakesh and showed her photos of snake charmers and monkeys climbing on her head. The dates that we'd bought on the square were passed around, as if we were at some Roman banquet.

Jason seemed in much better health and more relaxed. I noticed Alice place her hand on his thigh under the table. In fact, we all seemed more relaxed as if the time on land had reset the journey and we were starting afresh.

With a strong breeze blowing, the Moroccan coast was soon out of sight. Nicholas talked to his father, feigning an interest in cricket even if he didn't share his father's passion for it. Beth and Jane were chatting about some Moroccan pillows Beth had picked up in Essaouira. Charlie listened to Daisy as she spoke with great passion about how exciting she'd found Marrakesh and how she wanted to stop off there again the following year when they were passing. Maybe this trip could be salvaged and the remainder would be an enjoyable adventure.

As lunch was cleared away and the last of the bottles of wine were emptied, our party broke up. Alice and Jason headed off to their cabin for a 'lie down', while I headed off with Daisy up to the deck to sunbathe.

I'm not sure if it was the lunch or nervousness at being back on the boat, but I suddenly felt very sick. We were skimming across the water at a fair pace now, and every time we rose and fell between waves I sensed my lunch lurching around inside me. I closed my eyes, hoping the nausea would pass, but the more I tried to forget about it the more I felt like throwing up.

When Daisy put the box of dates under my nose, I could control myself no longer. I ran to the side of the boat and threw up, the wind whipping the bile along the side of the boat. I was sick again and again, first my lunch, then the rest of my breakfast. Finally there was nothing but painful retching.

Daisy was there by my side, a look of concern on her face. Yasmin came along and placed a hand on my back. 'Do you normally suffer from seasickness?' she asked.

As my stomach took a break from retching, I shook my head. 'I've been fine up until now.'

'Seasickness can be like that. Every time you step on a boat is the first time as far as seasickness goes. It doesn't normally last too long – only a day or so in my experience – unless you're very unlucky.'

A day or so? That couldn't be right. I had nothing left to bring up. My legs were already feeling weak.

'Let's sit down,' Yasmin said. 'I'll get a bowl for you and some water. Eat nothing. Don't lie down – if you can, sit up and watch the horizon. The fresh air and the horizon will help reset your system. There's nothing else that can be done.'

I sat in a chair at the front of the yacht, feet up on a storage box, watching the horizon as it bobbed up and down before me. I couldn't believe watching something not stay still was going to help my stomach settle, but after a while I noticed that the wretchedness was fading.

I sipped a little water, but the sickness returned almost immediately. Daisy sat with me, talking about something and nothing as I tried to concentrate on the horizon and swallow the nausea. I gripped the bowl and tried to think about anything other than the constant motion of the sea.

I dozed for a bit and was awoken by Alice, who was looking

at me with concern. 'Are you okay, sweetie?' she asked, looking flushed after her afternoon with Jason.

'Not really, but I'm feeling a bit better now.' I licked the salt off my lips and reached for the bottle of water. The sun was lower in the sky and I guessed I'd slept for some time. Daisy was nowhere to be seen, so I asked Alice to sit down beside me. 'How's Jason?' I asked.

'Well, I've tried to cheer him up but he's still down about everything that has gone on. To be honest, I'm worried about him. He's normally such an upbeat, positive man but now he seems to have the weight of the world on his shoulders.'

'Really? I was just thinking how good he looked when I saw him at lunch. It's the most relaxed I've seen him for a few days,' I said.

Alice shook her head. 'He may seem like it on the outside, but inside he's a bit of a mess. He cried after we had sex this afternoon and I couldn't console him. I've never seen him like this.'

'I'm so sorry, Alice. This trip seems to have been a real strain on a lot of people, Jason especially. At lunch he seemed much better, reinvigorated even. It just goes to show that you can't always read people.'

'He puts on a good front, but he's still very fragile and I don't know how to help him.'

'He seems strong, and I know you are. You will come through this. Try not to worry too much.'

'Thanks, Summer. You're right – everything will seem better tomorrow. Now, you need to look after yourself. Can I get you anything?'

'No, I'm okay. I think I'll stay here a little longer. Being outside seems to be better for me.'

The next couple of days were a bit of a blur. As we left the African coastline behind us, I spent much of my time in the shade on deck, unable to hold down food and drinking only water. Dry toast and biscuits were brought out to me but I couldn't face them. I was embarrassed to be so sick, although the others were sympathetic. How strange that seasickness should come on part of the way through the journey. Nobody else seemed to be affected, so food poisoning seemed unlikely. Yasmin put it down to us moving at speed now as we tried to make up for lost time.

On the third or fourth day, I'm not sure which, I awoke on the sun lounger that I'd made my bed just as the sun was setting. My eyes felt heavy, weighed down by the salty sea air that had dried on my skin. I hadn't slept well, but at least I'd gone twenty-four hours without throwing up. Despite that, every time I moved around the nausea returned. My stomach hurt constantly from straining my muscles.

I tried to lift myself up, but my arms seemed to have lost their strength. Beside me was a fresh glass of water, left by somebody who'd checked on me but had left me undisturbed. Behind me I heard laughter and voices, muffled by distance and the warm wind that was buffeting me. I took a sip then tried to raise myself from the chair again and took a few unsteady steps.

I stood for a moment, looking on as everyone sat around the dinner table. The meal was finished and the cheese board was out, together with the port. Alice seemed to be holding court, entertaining everyone with a story. Jason was sitting next to her wearing his burgundy-velvet dinner jacket; he appeared to be transfixed and was smiling as he watched her performance.

I thought Alice might be drunk. Her gestures were exaggerated and her movements clumsy, and the few words I caught sounded slurred. It was no surprise, really; meals rarely ended without someone being very drunk. As Alice went to sit down, she only just managed to hit the chair, stumbling badly and knocking into Charlie. He turned and said something to her, and she shook her head before Jason leant in and spoke.

Charlie helped Alice to her feet. She said something to the group in an exaggerated, flamboyant manner, then allowed Charlie to walk towards her cabin. Jason got up to help her, but Charlie placed a hand on his shoulder.

Jason's eyes kept flicking towards the cabin, as if he were deciding whether or not to go and check on his wife. Nobody else seemed overly concerned and the table returned to its conversation.

Chapter 33

After

S leeping so lightly had given me time to think as I drifted in and out of consciousness. Jason hadn't killed himself; I was sure of that. When I thought about who might have killed him and why, I had plenty of suspects. Almost everyone onboard had a motive, and all of the classics were there – revenge, jealousy, greed and fear. When everyone had a motive, motive alone wouldn't help me. The when and the how, that was what I needed to resolve.

That last night Jason had seemed fine to me, but Alice had said he wasn't coping well and she'd been worried about him. I hadn't seen him after dinner, but Daisy had told me he had gone to bed because he was concerned about Alice. Nobody reported seeing him after the meal yet, at some point between then and the early hours of the morning, he had a rope tied around his neck and he was left to be strangled behind the boat. Alice said Jason hadn't returned to the room and so must have gone to see someone after the meal. No one recalled seeing him, or at least they weren't saying.

As I pondered this, something nagged me, out of reach. There was something not right about this, and I needed to see the body again quickly. I realised that I was close to making an important connection.

I went in search of Yasmin; I needed to get another look inside that freezer. There was no resistance this time as she led me back down to the galley and unlocked the freezer door. I unzipped the body bag again and there was Jason, lying exactly as before in his shirt and dark trousers, looking undressed with only one shoe.

Looking more closely, I noticed that his shirt had not only lost a button, but it wasn't buttoned correctly: one of the buttons was in the wrong hole and there was an unused button hole at the bottom. I had what I needed, and I left.

Antigua was now fast approaching and we would arrive in just an hour. The police would be waiting for us. No doubt they would want to interview Yasmin and Mike, probably Alice as well, before deciding they had looked into Jason's death and settling on suicide. I knew who the killer was and had a pretty good idea how they'd done it. I just needed one final item to back up my theory.

I headed off to the cabins. Reaching Jason's cabin, I checked it was empty by knocking on the door. With no answer, I entered and went to the mirrored wardrobe in the corner, slid back the door and looked inside. At one end hung Jason's burgundy dinner jacket.

I sat on the bed for a minute, unsure of my next step. Satisfying myself who the killer was and how they'd done it was one thing; convincing some local cop on a holiday island that a millionaire's yacht contained a killer would be more difficult. An Englishman dead, at sea, far from the island – was that really worth the hassle to them? It was unlikely when suicide looked so obvious and was a tidy solution. No, I needed

155

a plan that would convince the police that they had a murder to deal with and that I'd found the killer.

I returned to my room and began to pack. I'd booked four nights in a hotel in Antigua and then I would be flying home. That didn't give me much time to organise things but, if I was lucky, it would give me the opportunity to put my plan into action.

I had two immediate issues to deal with. The first was to sow seeds of doubt with the police that Jason's death was a suicide, and fortunately I had Alice to help me with that. The second was a phone call back to the UK to talk to my producer. That would be more difficult, but it was essential to my plan and simply had to work.

Chapter 34

Before

It was my first night in my cabin after spending several days sleeping on deck to control my seasickness. I was woken early by heavy footsteps and raised voices. I could hear someone banging on doors and then a hysterical cry. I rolled out of bed and noticed through the porthole window that the yacht was just swaying gently in the swell; we were no longer moving.

I grabbed the dress I'd worn the day before from the floor and pulled it over my head. A scream made me jump, and I looked nervously out of the cabin up and down the corridor. At the far end towards the stairs that led to the rear deck, I saw the shadow of someone disappear up the staircase. Through the glass door to the rear deck I could see everyone outside, so I slid back the door and took the couple of steps up on to the stern deck.

I found a group huddled around something on the deck with Yasmin and Charlie leaning over it. There was a hushed silence. Everything stood still for me as I realised what they were looking at.

Alice was being supported by Mike, a look of stunned horror

on her face. Beth broke away from the group, went across to the rail and threw up. Then she sat on the edge of a sun lounger and rested her head on the handrail, looking pale even with her suntan.

I moved forward to see who was on the deck. As I stood between Jane and Nicholas, I looked down on Jason's face and brought a hand to my mouth to suppress an involuntary gasp.

He lay on the deck, still dressed as he'd been last night but missing a shoe. His body looked as you might expect a body to look after being in the water, but his face and neck made my stomach turn. A noose had pulled tightly around his throat and his neck had been constricted by the thick rope. The rope had been cut to reveal the deep trauma. His face was most disturbing: his boyish good looks were gone, his face transformed into a hideous death mask. One of his eyes was bulging and his skin was completely drained of blood.

I looked over to Alice then moved out of the circle around Jason across to her and took her in my arms. She was quivering as if she were frozen to the bone, calming and then trembling again. She put her head onto my shoulder and let out a sob, one that sent her body into a new fit of shakes.

'Let me take you inside.' I guided her towards her cabin. As I opened the door, she crumpled into my arms. I had to half carry her to her bedroom, where I lay her down and threw a sheet over her. I sat on the bed with her while she cried into my dress, wetting the material with her tears.

On the bedside table sat a box of sleeping pills. I leant across and lifted them up to look. They had been prescribed to Jason, presumably to help him sleep after the accident during the storm. 'Alice, take one of these. It acts as a sedative and it will help calm you down.'

She appeared to not have heard me. I released a pill from the packet and placed it on her tongue. She didn't resist, and I reached for a glass of water to help her wash it down.

I sat with her for some time, holding her hand. Her trembling became less frequent and her tears started to slow. As her breathing became shallower, she looked up at me and said, 'What just happened, Summer?'

I squeezed her hand, but I had no words of comfort. This all felt surreal, here on this yacht in the middle of the ocean with my old college friend, trying to comfort her after her husband's suicide. How had an adventure come to this?

'I wish we'd left this voyage in Morocco,' Alice said. 'You know Mike wanted to kick us off there? Beth talked him out of it, but I should have made that decision. I should have known my husband and that, with the money worries and the accidents, he would have been better off going home. I should have forced him to leave but he wanted to carry on, for me and for you,' Alice said.

'Don't blame yourself. You couldn't have known what was going to happen, and you have no way of knowing that things would have turned out differently if you'd left. It's tragic, but you can't criticise yourself.'

Alice began sobbing again. I stroked her hair out of her face as I felt her warm tears on my hand. Outside I heard Charlie talking to someone – it sounded like Mike. I could hear them discussing life insurance. How could they, at a time like this?

Chapter 35

After

I t was the first test of the England tour and the Sir Vivian
Richards Stadium was starting to fill up. Built only a
dozen years earlier for the cricket World Cup, it probably
sat empty for most of the year, but the two stands were now
coming to life.

There was a sea of England white shirts and union flags
draped over the stands. Around the rest of the ground were
grassy areas where temporary seating would have been placed
for the sold-out World Cup games. Now these areas were
being used by a few families and groups that had turned up
with picnics to enjoy a day of eating and drinking as a game of
cricket was played in the background.

The team and coaching staff knew Mike well; he was a
wealthy fan who spent much of the year following them around
the world, mingling with them at after-tour parties. We had a
private box halfway up one of the stands, an air-conditioned
room laid out with food and drink. Team staff and former
players dropped by to say hello to an obviously generous fan
whom they seemed genuinely to like.

Mike was in his element as he floated around enjoying the

attention he received from his cricket heroes, past and present. His Brummie accent and laughter filled the room.

There were two days left before I was due to fly out but, right now, things were looking awkward. Alice and I had managed to persuade the police that Jason's death might not be clear cut. Without evidence, the police clearly doubted our allegations but they were forced to open an initial investigation that had now been sent to a magistrate. He would review the case and decide if the death would be recorded as suicide or if a formal murder investigation needed to be opened.

Everyone onboard had been interviewed and given state-ments the day we arrived. Mike and the others were clearly not happy that Alice and I weren't following the line that Jason had killed himself, but that wasn't surprising. To suggest he hadn't was our polite way of saying that someone on board the yacht was a killer, willing to murder and cover it up.

Mike was close to the cricket team and planned to spend the next six months with them on their winter tour. Even the suggestion that he and his family were suspects in a murder case would result in him becoming persona non grata.

Daisy had told me he was fuming. He was already annoyed about arriving late and missing the pre-tour party, but his anger was made worse by having to be interviewed by the local police. He'd have dropped Alice and I like stones if he hadn't been scared we would make things worse for him by talking to the press. So instead he smiled at us through gritted teeth and brought us along to the match.

I had made sure that Alice hadn't had a chance to speak to me since we arrived. She kept looking for a chance to come over. As Daisy went off in search of lemonade, I stood by an enormous glass window looking down on the cricket; the match had started without me noticing. In here, behind the glass wall, we were strangely detached from the game below. The only sound that reached us was the radio commentary coming through the speakers. The crowd was quiet as they settled into the first of several dozen hours spread over five days.

I saw Alice watching us in the reflection of the glass. As Daisy left my side, she headed over. 'We need to talk. The police have gone quiet and I'm worried. I need to return to the UK with Jason, but I can't have everyone thinking it is suicide. At the same time, I can't be stuck here while they take their time. Did you not give them a suspect to focus on after all your investigations?'

I looked down at the cricket ground. On one of the grass areas the organisers had erected a large, shallow swimming pool. A few English fans were already cooling off from the morning heat.

'We can't talk here, it's too quiet,' I said. 'Let's go down to the pool and talk there. We'll have to go down separately, otherwise Daisy will join us.'

I went out while Alice stayed and watched the game. There was a small cheer from the crowd as someone made a run, evidently the first of the game. As I went down, I passed a TV cameraman and picked up the England cap beside him. I put it on my head to block the sun that was already hurting my head. I was wearing a short blue dress that wrapped around me, it's cotton as thin and light as possible without being transparent, yet I was still melting in the morning sun.

I kicked off my sandals and stepped into the pool. The water was cooler than the air, but still lukewarm. Around me, the English fans were enjoying the novelty of standing in a pool and watching cricket in the sun while their friends back home would be wrapped up in autumn jumpers.

Alice came up behind me and tapped me on the shoulder. 'Nice hat, Summer.'

'Thanks. I thought it would help me fit in and keep off the sun. I want to update you. I know how hard the past few days have been for you, but we haven't had a chance to be alone.'

'When you didn't say anything to me, I was worried you hadn't found any evidence.'

A cheer went up behind me and one of the England players came charging towards us, chasing a ball that was heading for the boundary. He slid to the ground at the last moment, scooping it up, jumping to his feet, turning and throwing it with perfect precision, all in one smooth, continuous movement. A cheer went up from the England fans.

'My only conclusion is that Jason was murdered. There's no evidence of suicide – no note, no suggestion that he was suicidal the night before. He wasn't happy and knew he'd upset a lot of people, but he gave no sign of being in such a desperate state of mind. The night before he died, I saw him laughing during the meal. He seemed at ease, not hours away from taking his own life. So the question is, who might have killed him? Sadly, the list of possible suspects is quite long. I need a bit more information before I can go to the police. What I need to know is how Jason met Beth. I keep hearing different stories.'

'I've told you this before. You'll need to ask Beth the details, but I doubt she'll be honest. Jason's not around to contradict her. As far as I know, Jason met Mike at a motor show and hit it off. Mike then introduced Jason to Beth.'

'I heard another story, that Jason met Beth first while he was down in the South of France, and maybe it wasn't a random meeting.'

'Why do you ask? Do you think Beth had something to do with Jason's death?'

'Beth? No. I think Beth was in love with Jason.' I tried to see Alice's eyes behind her shades. 'But more than that, I think you knew it and even encouraged it. In fact, I wouldn't be surprised if you didn't know from the start. It all feels a bit too convenient that Jason happened to run into the wife of a multi-millionaire, read the same book as her and love the same football team as her husband.'

'It would sound like that, wouldn't it, if that was what happened? I can see why you might think that, but you're wrong. The first I heard of Beth was when Jason told me he had a meeting lined up with a possible new client who was a football fan, and that he'd been invited to watch a game from his executive box. Jason was very open that he'd met Beth at some motor show and they had hit if off when he was there. She was just the wife of a business contact though.'

'I have this theory that I can't shake. Let me share it with you. I've pictured it all in my head. You and Jason were struggling for money. Work had dried up and he needed a client, one with enough money to save you. I can see you scouring *The Sunday Times* Rich List, looking for somebody with wealth but who wasn't too smart. Did you look for rich widows first, go through the list and circle possible targets? Were Mike and Beth your first choice or easier targets? I assume you checked them out – internet research to note their hobbies and interests, anything to give you a way in. How did you know Beth would be in Antibes, though? Was it via the charity she's patron of? Did you know she'd be there to give a speech?'

CHAPTER 35

Alice's smile turned into a laugh. 'You do have quite an imagination, Summer. That all sounds very clever on our part, snaring a rich client like that. It might even seem like something that I'd do, but Jason? Never. '

'That's the thing, I don't think Jason would have done it normally. But he adored you, and I imagine he'd do anything you asked. He was ambitious and, with you there pushing him, he'd have found it hard to say no. Did he resist? Did you have to wear him down?'

'You're being ridiculous. I think the heat has made you lightheaded. Jason didn't need pushing into anything. He met Mike and then was friendly with Beth. Was I suspicious of the relationship between Beth and Jason? At times, but it was more concern on my part. Beth had become obsessed with Jason. She messaged him constantly, inviting him to events, conferences and parties. She'd had a fiction in her head that she was going to leave Mike for him.' Alice paused for a moment. 'If Beth thought Jason had targeted her, used her to get to Mike, however ridiculous that might seem it could have given her or Mike the motive to kill him.'

'I had considered that. Beth would be very hurt if she knew she'd been used like that. In fact, I think she probably does know, but however they met, Beth fell for Jason and there is no way she would have harmed him. So what happened in Morocco?'

Alice adjusted her glasses as she looked back towards the room where Beth could be seen, glass in hand, talking to a woman I didn't recognise.

'He went to talk to her the first night we were there. He told her to back off in no uncertain terms. When she persisted, he threatened to tell Mike. She flew off the handle, full "woman

165

scorned". Jason was scared.'

'The Beth I saw that evening was upset more than angry. I don't know what exactly went on between those two, but I believe Beth loved Jason and would never have hurt him. So that leaves the question: if not Beth, then who killed Jason?'

Alice held my look. 'Well, at least you believe he was killed. That's all I wanted really, to be able to say to his family that he didn't take his own life.'

'Not forgetting the life insurance money?'

'How do you mean?'

'Life insurance doesn't pay out when somebody commits suicide. It wasn't only Mike's money Jason was investing, was it? Everything you had was invested as well. Not only was Jason going to lose Mike as a client, but his reputation was also tarnished. You faced financial ruin due to one bad investment. You borrowed money to increase your investment, leveraged up so that you could maximise the profits. The entire investment was wiped out and probably left you with debts as well. Hopefully you were smart and borrowed the money through his company so there was no personal liability, but the business would still be bankrupt and you'd be wiped out financially.'

'I didn't know that about the insurance,' said Alice, her face perfectly composed.

Chapter 36

Before

Alice was now breathing deeply, so I carefully moved her off my chest and tucked her under the sheets.

I headed back up but found the deck nearly empty. Jason's body had already been moved and the area mopped down. The rope had gone. Only Yasmin remained, sitting on the guard rail, her back to me as she looked out to sea. She was smoking, the smell from her strong French cigarette reaching across the deck. She hadn't heard my approach, so I gently touched her shoulder. She turned to look at me. There were no tears, but her dark eye makeup was smudged and she looked as if she'd been crying.

'How's Alice?' she asked.

'I gave her a sleeping tablet to try and calm her down. I don't know if that was the best idea. I'm really not sure what's appropriate for something as awful as this.'

'Sleep can never be a bad thing. You're a good friend and she'll need you now.'

'I know. Unfortunately, I've been through a similar shock and it took me a long time to recover from it. Alice is strong, though, and she'll get through. I'm sure of that.' I climbed over the railing and sat beside her, looking out at the great expanse behind us. Time passed as we sat there, the yacht not travelling but being gently lifted and lowered by the ocean.

'Have you contacted the police?' I asked.

'Mike and I contacted the coastguard. We're now in international waters, so jurisdiction becomes tricky. As Jason is English, the British will want to be involved, but the *Althea* is registered in the Bahamas and their police would normally investigate. It's difficult. As we're so far out, we've been advised to carry on to Antibes and let the police there perform the formalities since Jason took his own life.'

We both sat and pondered the enormity of what had happened this morning. Then Yasmin added, 'I'm sorry for your loss, Summer. Were you very close to Jason?'

'No. We only met on the journey down to meet you for the first time. I haven't seen or heard much from Alice in recent years. The invitation was a real surprise, and I wondered if my availability was the key to my being here.'

'Really? That surprises me. I thought you and Alice were very close.'

'I'd say we were close once upon a time but, in hindsight, we were probably not as close as I thought. This trip has probably made me realise just how different we are. It's funny how a shared history can give you a false feeling of friendship. You're thrown together with people due to circumstances rather than a true connection.' I thought back over the distant relationship I had with Alice.

'I hope Alice has some good friends back home,' Yasmin said. 'She's going to need support for some time. Killing yourself is so cruel to those left behind. Jason seemed like a good man to me, not one who would be so selfish. But you never really know people, even those closest to you.'

'No. It leaves you shaken when someone behaves in such an unexpected way.'

'Last night he seemed relaxed, *enjoué* at times. I don't know the English word for this – jolly, maybe?'

'I wasn't here when he was brought on board. Did you find him? What happened?'

Yasmin took one last long drag on her cigarette and flicked the butt into the ocean. 'I noticed the rope tied around the flagpole and was curious what it was doing there. I tried to pull it in, but it was too heavy while we were moving. I could see something in the water and immediately got a bad feeling. I called for assistance from the others and set about lowering the sails so we could stop moving too fast. Mike came, and then Nicholas, Jane and Charlie. We pulled the rope in. It was only as the body got close to us that I realised who it was...'

She wasn't crying, but her voice was cracking as she tried to describe to me how she'd lifted Jason from the water. The rope had cut so deeply into his neck that she had to dig into him with a knife to cut him free.

'How were the others?' I asked.

'You never know how you're going to react to something like that. As they came out on deck, the silence was eerie. Nobody spoke – the shock was too intense for us to process it to begin with. We all jumped when we heard Alice scream as she slumped into Mike's arms. It's not something I ever want to witness again.'

Chapter 37

After

'In the cabin, just after Jason was found, we both overheard Charlie talking about insurance. I remember thinking how disrespectful the conversation was. It was only later that I realised what that meant for you – although it's irrelevant now because I know it wasn't suicide.'

As I spoke, Alice's eyes opened.

I continued. 'So, it wasn't Beth who killed him, we can be sure of that. Jane is a strange one, though. She loves Mike, always has. She loves him more than Beth does. But love is a strange emotion that's hard to find. When you *have* found it, not much can break it. Even though Mike is clearly fond of Jane, he seems to have never loved her in return. Most women would have walked away, but not her. Just being around Mike seems to be enough for her, and her poor, hapless husband has to turn a blind eye. What tangled love lives these people lead – no one truly happy, everyone pining for love and attention from someone who has their eyes elsewhere.

'The question I asked myself was if Jane had a motive for killing Jason. She certainly had strong suspicions about Beth and Jason, and she believed they were having an affair. Jane would do anything to protect Mike, but you'd think an affair between Jason and Beth would play into her hands. Jane has demonstrated how much she loves Mike by not telling him her suspicions about Beth. Telling Mike might have destroyed his marriage and left the door open for her but, to her credit, she's kept quiet to protect him. That seems like true love to me.'

Alice was listening intently when a man in an England shirt kicked water at his friend. We both instinctively jumped back to avoid the shower of water. Alice's arm knocked off my cap but I saved it expertly from the water. I took a deep breath and closed my eyes for a moment after such a close call.

'Nicholas, though – he's one strange character. For a long time, I thought he had a problem with me and was an arrogant son of a bitch who saw Jason standing between him and his father, preventing him getting the investment he wanted. He's a bit of a spoilt brat, but I've learnt that his aloofness with me was down to his childlike inability to talk to women he liked. It took me a while to realise that – I thought he hated me from the off. When it dawned on me that he wasn't an arse but immature, I looked at him differently. Could he have killed Jason? He had the opportunity. He let Jason almost drown when they were scuba diving, and he was up on the deck the night Jason was hit. So was it third time lucky for Nicholas?'

'So you think it was Nicholas?' Alice interrupted.

'It's his motive that's the problem. Jason spoke to Mike and advised him against investing in Nicholas's venture, but Mike was never going to invest in it anyway. He made that clear, and it sounds like it wasn't the first time Nicholas had come up with a "sure fire" business idea that just needed a million quid to get it going. No, Jason was a nuisance but not enough of a block to Nicholas's plans.'

171

'What about the money lost in the investment Jason made? Surely that would be enough for Nicholas to feel aggrieved?' Alice asked.

'Aggrieved, yes, but not homicidal. At the end of the day, it wasn't his money. Look at what he has. It's not like he's living a bad life, and it's not the first time he has asked his dad for money and been turned down. I get the feeling that Nicholas wants a shortcut to success, a quick path to running a business that money can buy him. He has grown up expecting certain privileges, and he rejects the idea of the hard work that Mike wants to see him put in. I suspect Mike would fund him, but only when Nicholas has put in the initial hard graft and demonstrated he is serious and committed.'

I turned to look at the cricket match. An over had just been completed and the players were moving to new positions on the field. 'Nicholas is still living in his father's shadow, riding on his coat tails. He's in his twenties and still goes on holiday with them every year. Look at him up there in the executive box, drinking champagne and watching cricket. Mike needs to cut him off a little, force him to start his business with nothing and prove his worth. He won't be short of investors if he can prove himself.'

Alice moved to stand beside me. We both looked out across the ground and up into the executive box where we make out the others mingling with friends and hangers-on who had joined them.

'I don't know about Nicholas. He has a temper and I think he makes a very good suspect. He certainly had a motive, especially if you're right and Jason cheated on me with Beth.' Alice leaned in and lowered her voice as she spoke the last words.

'Oh, he has a motive alright but not a strong one. And a motive doesn't make him a killer. Resorting to murder is a desperate act, a last resort when all else seems hopeless. Jason wasn't really a threat to Nicholas, and any damage he'd done was in the past and not worthy of revenge.

'On the other hand, Mike had a reason to seek revenge. A lot of men would react violently if they found out their wife was carrying on behind their back and look at ways to hurt their rival. Would they lure them onto a luxury holiday so they could murder them? Would they invite their wife and her friend along as well? Seems pretty unlikely, doesn't it? So if jealousy were a motive, that means Mike found out about an affair while on this trip. I'm unsure if he knew or even suspected that something was going on, or if he's a cuckold who was able to turn a blind eye to his wife's behaviour, so long as she stayed with him. If he found out about them during this vacation, he's hidden it well. No, jealousy doesn't seem to be his motive.

'Losing millions would be an understandable motive if it left him destitute and he was forced to give up this lifestyle that both he and Beth enjoy. But it didn't quite go that far. Jason seems to have got out of the contracts before the losses became unsustainable – well, unsustainable for someone with eye-watering wealth. I suspect Jason lost between ten and twenty million, more money than most people ever dream about. I can see that hurt Mike, but I imagine the loss can be managed. Mike sold the business for about seventy million. He and Beth have clearly spent a lot since then, but I doubt they're down to their last forty million, even after the disastrous investment.'

I turned to look at Alice, studying her deep brown eyes.

'Knowing that must hurt you, Alice. Mike lost, but he didn't lose everything while you and Jason lost it all.'

Alice gave a wry smile. 'We lost a lot, I admit, but nothing we wouldn't have bounced back from if Jason hadn't been ripped from me. It's only Jason that I care about. The money is secondary to having my soulmate taken from me. You know how that feels, Summer.'

Her words brought all those feelings of loss flooding back and I grabbed the handrail to steady myself. I swayed for a moment before grounding myself again and looking at her. Her face was as cool and composed as ever.

I adjusted my cap as I studied Alice. The match and the sounds of the crowd around me disappeared as I concentrated my attention on her.

'I thought at one point that Yasmin might be involved in Jason's death,' I mused. 'She always seemed to be around when bad things happened to him. She was inflating her invoices or covering up for someone else. Jason believed it was her and challenged her about it. But it was peanuts in the grand scheme of things, and would Yasmin kill to protect her job? No. She's an experienced captain and will have no trouble finding work elsewhere, even without a reference from Mike. Mike would never involve the police over the invoices – they were small beer and Yasmin would know that. No, Yasmin didn't know Jason before the trip and really had no reason to kill him.

'He was murdered, though, that much is obvious. But I kept asking myself who would actually benefit from his death. The only person I hadn't looked at was you, Alice. Why would I? Had you not come to me that morning, I would have assumed that tragically Jason took his own life due to the guilt of losing Mike's money and the shame of losing yours. But the more I looked at everyone else, the more I kept coming back to the one person who had both motive and opportunity. You!' I jabbed my finger at her.

Alice laughed, not fazed at all by my accusation. 'Yes, of course! I commit murder then ask an investigative journalist to look into the case.' Her voice dripped sarcasm. 'That wouldn't be a very smart thing to do, now would it?'

'Oh, I don't know. Maybe you thought it would give you an alibi and you'd been careful to cover your tracks. It could have worked, but you made the same mistake as others have done – you underestimated me.

'Being underestimated is my greatest strength. When I talk to people, they let down their guard. They don't see me as a threat. Even you, Alice. You've known me for years, yet you believed that you were smarter than me and I was some airhead who was always one step behind you.

'Have you actually seen any of my shows, watched how I lull corrupt business owners into a false sense of security? Maybe you have and assumed it was luck that they revealed what they most wanted hidden. You're manipulative and conniving, but you lack the smarts to realise you're not the brightest person in the room. And even if you were, that doesn't make everyone else a fool. Your greed has got you and Jason into trouble. Your ruthless pursuit of wealth means you'd do anything to avoid losing it all, even temporarily.'

Alice laughed but, as she swept back her hair, I sensed a hesitation. 'You're funny sometimes. I asked you because I thought you would identify the killer. I didn't imagine that you'd get desperate and attack me, though. Okay, humour me. So how did I become a stone-cold husband killer?'

I could feel myself trembling, standing in the pool and trying to stay cool but feeling the effects of the sun. I should have found a shady spot to do this but, other than in the crowded stands, shade was in short supply.

I took a deep breath. 'I believe you persuaded Jason to target Beth in the South of France. With his charisma and good looks, you knew this older and very wealthy married woman would fall for his charm. You handpicked Beth as the target, researched her based on information in *The Sunday Times* Rich List or something similar. She's an attractive older woman married to a man with thinning hair and a beer belly. I imagine you were with Jason in the South of France, pointed her out, set the trap.

'You knew Jason wouldn't sleep with her, or you didn't care if he did. The money was the goal, and you were ready to sacrifice your man for money. You probably married Jason thinking he *had* money and, when it turned out he didn't and his family had borrowed to send him to private schools, you must have been gutted. Jason was posh, but it was with a small "p".

The thing is, I know the one thing you desire above all else is wealth and the security and status it brings. After finding out that Jason had lost all of the money – your money – you decided to cut your losses, go for the insurance payout. No doubt you'll go hunting for a new husband, one who is better equipped to give you what you crave.

'You planned for Jason to have an accident, but both attempts failed and you grew more desperate and more careless. Life insurance pays out on death but not suicide, and you hadn't thought of that. You overheard Charlie talking outside the cabin after I gave you the sedative. How you must have panicked before the drugs finally knocked you out.

'All those years of acting class were called into action – the crocodile tears and acting drunk. Yes, that last night, that final meal when you went to bed so drunk you could hardly walk and fell asleep in a drunken stupor. It was a fantastic performance and very convincing. No one would have suspected that you could be involved in Jason's death because you passed out after an evening of drinking.'

Alice's cold, confident face was starting to droop and her smile was no longer relaxed. I could see I was getting to her. 'Jason never came back to our room and I never saw him alive again after that meal. This might be an amusing fantasy for you, but it hurts me.'

She suddenly burst into tears, her shoulders rising and falling as her whole body shook. The people standing around us turned away from the cricket to stare. God, she was good. If I hadn't already known her, this performance might have made me doubt myself and retract my words. She reached out to put her arms around me, but I took a step back and carried on.

'Jason came back to your room, just as the others said he had,' I continued. 'He hung up his jacket in the wardrobe, got undressed and slipped into bed beside you. He had no idea that the one person he adored and would have done anything for had put plans in motion to kill him.

'He'd drunk a fair bit with his meal, and probably fell asleep quickly. You waited patiently, watching him sleep, probably snoring with the alcohol running through him. When the ship was quiet, you woke him and gave him a couple of sleeping pills. In his state, Jason wouldn't have questioned you. He'd have swallowed them down and fallen straight back to sleep. With the alcohol and pills, he must have been dead to the world within the hour. So you waited again as he fell into unconsciousness. Did you use that time to reflect on what you were about to do? Or did you look down at him with disgust, a failure who had lost you everything, no longer useful but a burden that would prevent you from getting the life you needed?'

Alice slapped me hard, forcing me to stumble backwards and fall into the water. A couple of people nearby offered their hands to help me up, not realising that I hadn't merely slipped on the bottom of the pool. Alice was turning and walking away, ready to leave me there drenched.

I stepped forward and grabbed her, my wet hand pulling back her shoulder. 'You can't walk away from what you did, Alice. You killed him. You took his unconscious body and dressed him again, but you messed up his shirt buttons in your haste. You dragged him onto the deck, sat him on the edge of the boat, tied a rope around his neck and attached it to the flagpole. Did he stay unconscious the whole time, or was he aware that something was very wrong? Was he awake enough to resist you or plead with you? Did you kiss him before you pushed him?'

This time Alice really went for me. Her composure was completely gone and she swung out, half catching me with a punch. This time I did slip and fell backwards into the water as Alice threw herself on top of me. She used her superior strength to hold me there as I desperately held onto my hat.

'You think you're so clever and worked it all out,' she snarled. 'But no one will believe that the grieving widow who went to bed drunk somehow murdered her husband. Mike is the obvious suspect. Even if they find no evidence against him, the case will be left open and I'll get my money,' she shouted, even as hands were dragging her off me.

Her eyes were wild and blazing as she shook them off. As I was helped to my feet, she came into my face and looked me in the eyes. 'And yes, just between us, that useless idiot pleaded to me. Half asleep, he begged me not to do it, even though he'd no idea what I was about to do. It was quick and merciless, and I felt no remorse, only anger when I realised I wouldn't get the insurance money owed to me. But don't worry, I'll tell the cops Mike threatened him, promised revenge. Even if they never press charges, Jason's death will go down as suspicious and I'll get my life back on track – the grieving widow out to find the man of her dreams!'

I pushed her away, not wanting her face that close to me. She really was a bitch who would stop at nothing to get what she wanted. I pulled off my cricket hat and turned it inside out for her to see. I pulled out a tiny microphone from behind the three lions emblem and held it up.

'Thank you for the interview, Alice. Very revealing. If you could just turn to the side a little, the camera there can get a close-up of your face as it dawns on you that not only have you just confessed to murder, you've helped me produce my next documentary, one that will be the highlight of my career to date. The police have already found traces of the sleeping tablet in Jason's blood. It's not enough on its own to prove it was murder, but with your confession they'll have all they need.'

Alice stood, her face contorted in confusion as she looked around her and spotted that one of the camera crews wasn't focused on the match but pointing a camera directly at us. The realisation that she'd been outsmarted had a swift physical effect on her: her legs buckled and she sank down into the pool. The fans around us were now ignoring the game as they watched her slip back into the water and close her eyes. Two police officers arrived, took her by the arms and lifted her to her feet.

'Alice, before you go, I want to leave you with a thought to ponder over in jail. The irony is, while most people still believe life insurance companies don't pay out in the case of suicide, times have changed. Now they often do, depending on the circumstances. You almost committed the perfect crime. If you hadn't overheard the conversation Charlie was having and panicked, the insurance could well have paid out and you would have got away with it.'

There before me stood the real Alice. She wasn't acting now as the water glinted on her beautiful dark skin. She looked towards the sun, realising that her days of freedom and privilege were over for a very long time.

Chapter 38

Epilogue

The awards arrived and my star rating rose with them. The film of my confrontation with Alice became global news, and we turned the whole murder and confession into an hour-long documentary that might even be nominated for an Emmy.

Even without the admiration that I received for the film, I would have been pleased to see Jason get justice. Alice is still in a jail cell in Antigua, fighting extradition back to the UK to face murder charges. During her time there, she's gone from outright denial through accusations that she was framed, to claiming it was all fake news. Currently she is saying that she'd had a breakdown after the financial losses she suffered at Jason's hands, and remembers nothing of the night he died.

I have plans to interview her again for a follow-up film. She still believes she is smarter than me and can win public sympathy, so you might get to see that soon.

The day after that showdown in Antigua, I flew back to the UK. The police had helped me set up the whole confession from Alice and they had everything they needed, so I was allowed to leave.

I haven't seen Mike and Beth since. They continued the cricket tour throughout the winter as they had planned. Jane and Charlie went with them. I'm still in touch with Daisy and we speak occasionally; she's invited me to visit her at her new school in California next time I'm there. I might well take her up on it one day – she is such a sweet girl.

Nicholas waited until after I'd left to ask me out for a date. His invitation arrived in an email the week I returned to London. I was pleased to hear that he'd decided to start his business without the massive investment he'd wanted from his dad, but I had no intention of going out for dinner with him. Nicholas wants money to give him status and power. I've seen how money can bring pleasure but also how destructive it can be, and I'm not interested in anyone for whom money is their driving force.

I've started filming my new series and it's created quite a buzz. At the moment I'm the bright new thing enjoying my moment of fame. The only downside is that investigating financial wrongdoing has lost a little of its fascination. Maybe I need to keep my eye out for something more exciting. Something like a murder...?

Acknowledgement

Many thanks go to the following: To my early first-draft reader, Jane, whose words of praise kept me going early on. To Josh Green, my mum, and especially Ellen Coomber, whose invaluable feedback helped shape the second draft. To those friends for whom I was too scared to share the novel but who believed in me throughout. To Pippa for helping me to come up with a fitting murder, as well as being a wonderful mother. To Henry Sanford and all the amazing staff at AB who have given me so much encouragement and space to finish my novel. To Sue Coghlan for her amazing cover illistration. Finally, to my editor, Karen Holmes, who made my day when she told me how much she was loving the book and for helping to polish and craft the final version.

About the Author

Having run a number of book clubs for years, I wanted to write a book in the style of the books that members always loved, escapist page-turners and feel-good contemporary fiction. I use my experiences spent travelling to enrich my stories, giving each book an authentic insight to a different life. I now make Bristol my home, where I continue to run a book club while trying to avoid being too distracted by my favourite authors as I craft my next story.